Drowning in Broad Daylight

Also by Montana Carr

Beyond the Scent of Sugar: A Memoir by Billie River

Marti Starova Erotic Thrillers

Coming Soon!

Shadow Work (Book 2) – September 26, 2025

Rain-Soaked (Book 3) – November 5, 2025

Almost *(Book 4)* - January 16, 2026

The Familiar Dark (Book 5) - March 11, 2026

Drowning in Broad Daylight

A Marti Starova Erotic Thriller Book 1

Montana Carr

Northshore Noir Press

DROWNING IN BROAD DAYLIGHT. A Marti Starova Erotic Thriller Book 1. Copyright © 2025 by Montana Carr. All rights reserved.

Northshore Noir Press and the Northshore Noir logo are copyright and used with permission.

Northshore Noir Press
Toronto, Canada
www.northshorenoir.com

ISBN: 978-1-998648-19-1

eBook ISBN: 978-1-998648-20-7

For more information visit: northshorenoir.com

Contents

Chapter 1

"Where the fuck are my cigarettes?" Marti's voice cut through the office like a gunshot.

"Top left drawer," Lori called from the other room, way too fucking smug about it.

Marti yanked it open, rifling past crumpled receipts and old case notes until her fingers brushed the pack. Half-empty. Of course. She shook one out, jammed it between her lips, and reached for her lighter. Nothing. Christ. She checked every pocket twice before shoving a hand through her already-mussed hair.

Her office felt like a relic of a past that never existed: Cyberpunk Detective, Now with Extra Poor Life Choices. The cracked leather chairs sulked in the corners, worn and abandoned, their usefulness long forgotten. Her mahogany desk was buried under enough printouts and file stacks to trigger an audit. A forgotten Slip Drive laid somewhere beneath the mess. There was a burner phone tucked in the corner; its old-school design seemed like a joke, except it was too old to track and therefore priceless.

Her name, Marti Starova, Private Investigator, in gold lettering on the office door because people had certain expectations. They would walk in, see Lori Harring, the stereotypical beautiful blonde bombshell of a secretary, and then become bitterly disappointed when they laid eyes on Marti.

Tough shit.

The news feeds ran on her holo-tab flickered with alerts: corruption in neon pixels, stories told through flashing images more than words. The headlines barely needed to be written. Just the grim faces of politicians caught in scandal and missing persons reports that overlapped, fed through the feeds, reminding Falls City it was falling apart.

Marti looked out the office window. Five floors up. Just high enough to still smell the dumpsters, feel the traffic and hear the screams. Not high enough to see past a single building.

Neon flickered outside her window, light smeared across rain-slick pavement where gutter water mixed with God-knew-what else. The city never slept, never stopped humming its slow, rotting song beneath all that glitter and grime.

"Another thrilling adventure in mediocrity," Marti muttered around her unlit cigarette, slumping into her chair with an exhale that mixed exhaustion and disgust.

"Mediocrity is what you make of it." Lori's voice came from the doorway, warm but laced with something knowing, as if her patience made Marti want to crawl out of her own skin or push Lori against the nearest wall and kiss her just to shut her up.

Marti snorted, flicking at her empty lighter before tossing it across the desk. "That so?" She traced the jagged skyline through the window. "Seems to me we're just hamsters on a fucking wheel, Lori, running 'til we drop for what? A couple bucks? A black eye? Maybe one good night before it all turns to shit again?"

Lori shrugged and stepped inside like she belonged here, which she did because she was the secretary. "Beats stopping."

"Does it?" Marti shot back, sharp enough to cut glass as she leaned forward, elbows on knees. "Maybe stopping's the only way off this ride."

"Yeah?" Lori nudged aside a stack of files and perched on the edge of Marti's desk like she had all the time in the world, as if she wasn't standing in someone else's slow-motion wreckage and refusing to move out of the way. "And then what?"

Marti didn't have an answer for that. Just an old ache lodged deep in places she'd learned to ignore years ago. Her gaze drifted until it landed on something half-hidden near the papers: sleek, silver, whispering promises she didn't need spoken aloud. Shadow inhalers looked too pretty for something that ruined lives so thoroughly.

She reached for it without thinking. Stopped herself just as fast. Fingers curled into a fist instead, nails biting into her palm as if pain could replace temptation.

Lori didn't say anything this time. Just waited until Marti sighed through gritted teeth and leaned back again like it didn't matter either way.

"Forward," Marti muttered, voice dry as old whiskey and twice as bitter as she ground out an unlit cigarette against the desk edge instead of lighting it up like she wanted to. "Moving forward."

"Maybe it's time to stop letting this city chew you up and spit you out." Lori's voice was soft, her eyes full of something Marti didn't want to name. "You've still got fight left in you. Don't let your demons win."

"Demons," Marti scoffed, flipping the inhaler between her fingers before setting it down like it burned. "Funny. I like it when they eat me. They just don't have the decency to stay full."

Lori crossed her arms, undeterred. "Ignoring them doesn't make them disappear. Eventually, they catch up."

"Thanks for the therapy session," Marti said, turning away from the window. "I'll be sure to write you a glowing Falls Talk review."

Lori smirked as if she knew something Marti didn't. "Not looking for five stars, just trying to keep you upright."

Marti exhaled something close to a laugh. "Optimism is a disease."

"And yet here I am, terminal." Lori bumped Marti's arm with her elbow before stepping back toward the desk. "Now, if you're done drowning in self-loathing, we've got work to do. The city isn't going to save itself."

The glow of the computer screen cast everything in sickly blue light. The old machine wheezed as she plugged in the camera: another relic from better days. The lens had once captured murder scenes and crime lords; now it dealt in cheaper betrayals.

She flicked through the images: shadows draped over tangled limbs and desperate hands gripping at things not meant for them. A husband who thought he was careful but wasn't as clever as he believed. Mrs. Fischer had suspected; now she'd know for sure.

With a few adjustments, Marti sharpened the frames, pulling detail from darkness with surgical precision. A face half-hidden became unmistakable. A wedding ring caught the light in just the right way: undeniable proof that promises meant nothing under neon haze and cheap motel sheets.

"Lori!" Her voice cut through the quiet like a gunshot.

Footsteps. Then Lori was leaning over her shoulder, close enough that Marti could feel warmth radiating off her skin.

"What have you got?"

Marti smirked and tapped the screen. "Mr. Fischer being a very bad boy."

Lori's eyes widened as she scanned the shots. "Holy shit, you literally watched them screw?"

"It lasted three minutes," Marti said, taking a sip of coffee before adding, "Four if we're generous about foreplay."

Lori let out a low whistle. "Brutal."

Marti dragged the damning images into an already-bulging case folder and started drafting an email, brief and detached, but stopped short of hitting send. She never handed over evidence before confirming client surety first; rule number one in this line of work was simple: make sure they want what you're about to give them.

With a sigh, she minimized the draft and leaned back in her chair, stretching stiff muscles as she eyed the blurred figures on her screen one last time. Another night in this city: another secret waiting to burn everything down.

Marti rolled her neck, joints cracking like static, and glanced at the inhaler sitting next to her keyboard. Shadow stared back, patient as ever.

Fuck it.

She grabbed the metal cylinder, pressed it to her lips, and inhaled deep. The burn hit first: sharp, acrid. Then came the crash, a full-body sigh as Shadow flooded her system. The office dimmed around the edges, as if reality itself had decided to back off for a minute.

Warmth spread through her limbs, heavy and sweet, numbing the sharp angles of exhaustion. Her nerves dulled, tension unwound. The air itself tasted different: thicker, richer, as if she could sink her teeth into it and swallow oblivion whole. Colors deepened. Sound softened. Time stretched like taffy.

Her mind drifted loose from its moorings, buoyed by euphoria, floating near blissful detachment. Thoughts unraveled in slow spirals; memories, ideas, nonsense tangled with clarity in a way that almost made sense for once.

Shadow promised everything: a break, a breath, a fucking moment of peace in a city that never let up.

But peace was a cheap lie with an expensive price tag. And Marti already owed too much.

The high smoothed out into something manageable, edges softened but not gone, and she blinked herself back into focus.

Right. Business now.

Mrs. Fischer's name glowed on the screen like a bad omen, though Marti knew the truth was that she was the bad part of it. Her thumb tapped dial.

Marti exhaled. "This is Marti Starova," she said, keeping it cool despite the lingering haze in her head. "Your husband? We've got him."

Mrs. Fischer didn't miss a beat: "You better have bulletproof evidence, Marti! I can't believe that cheating bastard! I need to nail his ass to the wall in divorce court."

Marti smirked and nudged the case folder with her knuckles. "Oh, I've got proof." She flicked through the incriminating photos on her screen: time-stamped, crystal clear, damning as hell. Mr. Fischer in bed with someone who was not his wife and very much blonde. "You're looking at a solid payday in the divorce settlement."

"Good," Mrs. Fischer snapped, sharp enough to cut glass but shaking under it all if you knew how to listen right, which Marti did. "Thank you, Marti; you're a life-saver."

Marti leaned forward and hit send on the email draft: attachments included, no refunds accepted. She lit a cigarette as she propped her feet up on the desk. "It's what I do," she muttered around the smoke before dropping the call and tossing her phone aside.

Outside, sirens wailed somewhere distant: a song this city never stopped singing. Lori's voice drifted from the adjoining room:

"You getting high again?"

Marti smirked and took another drag before answering.

"Been there, done that."

Marti exhaled smoke toward the ceiling, watching it curl like a ghost looking for an escape. She flicked ash onto a week-old case file; printing everything was a habit from her days with Falls City Police. She spun her chair toward the office door.

"Lori, get in here."

A beat, then the shuffle of shoes against cheap carpet. Lori leaned in, one brow raised, half amused, half bracing for impact.

Marti gestured at the monitor. "We're padding Fischer's bill. Add another $2,500."

Lori's expression didn't change. "Feeling generous today?"

"Feeling underpaid." Marti stubbed out her cigarette in an empty coffee cup. "She's walking away from that marriage with a settlement big enough to buy this whole fucking building. I deserve a cut for sitting through those surveillance tapes. You ever see a man sweat through silk sheets? Because I have, and I can't unsee it."

"There's no coming back from that," Lori said, shuddering. Then she grinned. "Before I forget: I'm taking the afternoon off."

Marti tipped her head back and closed her eyes. "Do I even want to ask?"

"City Council's trying to ban the queer flag from government buildings. Again." Lori folded her arms, her weight shifting to one hip. "I'm going to remind them we exist."

"Election year?" Marti drawled.

"Bingo." Lori smirked. "Every four years like clockwork, the moral panic machine starts churning." Her expression softened. "Come with me?"

"Nah." Marti waved her off. "Go be queer enough for both of us."

"I always am." Lori tapped her fingers on the doorframe before heading to her desk, invoices forming in her head.

Marti watched her go, then slumped in her chair with a sigh that felt like surrender. Once, she would've been on the front lines: megaphone in one hand, zip-tie bruises on both wrists. Those days felt like someone else's life now. The fight still lived beneath the nicotine and drugs; it just wasn't hers anymore.

Outside, neon lights smeared across rain-slick pavement while Falls City hummed its usual dirge; car horns, distant sirens, muffled yelling that could've been laughter or worse. Marti let it wash over her as exhaustion crept in like high tide, pulling her under before she could think better of it.

* * *

The clock read too-late-into-fuck-it when Marti surfaced from sleep with a grunt and a crick in her neck that screamed poor life choices. Leather stuck to sweat-damp skin as she swung her legs over the couch and scrubbed at her eyes, trying to remember when she'd passed out and whether Shadow had played a part in it.

Probably.

She blinked until the room settled around her: same cluttered desk, same empty takeout containers threatening a takeover. She reached for the cigarette pack beside last night's unfinished coffee.

A voice cut through the static in her head.

"Rough night?"

Lori stood in the doorway as if a smirk had become flesh and bone.

Marti lit up instead of answering.

"You were dead to the world for hours," Lori added, stepping inside without waiting for an invitation.

Marti exhaled smoke and eyed Lori over it. "And yet you survived without me."

"Barely."

Lori wandered closer under false pretenses, grabbing a file off Marti's desk, but lingered for a delicious view.

Marti took another drag and pretended not to notice.

Lori grinned like she knew better.

Maybe she did.

"Am I not allowed to sleep?"

"Sure you are," Lori said, flipping through the stolen file as if it contained anything she cared about. "But you didn't leave the office. I figured I should check before you started to stink worse than you already do."

"Hilarious." Marti rolled her eyes, the irritation tempered by something close to fondness. "Now, if you don't mind, I have work to do."

"Work" was a generous term. Once, Marti had been someone: badge, commendations, enough grit to chew bullets and spit out justice. Then came the mistake. Then drugs. Now she was a PI with enough bad habits to serve as a walking cautionary tale.

Lori sighed as if giving up, but she didn't leave. Instead, she let her gaze roam over Marti's office; the chaos of cigarette burns and half-empty coffee cups and case files buried under takeout containers.

"I'll be outside," she said, dropping the file back onto the mess and heading for the door.

Marti waited until she was alone before pushing herself upright with a groan. Her desk fought back when she reached it: a knee slammed into wood, an elbow knocked a pen to the floor. Somewhere in the wreckage sat Augmented Reality glasses that hadn't worked in years but still made itself useful as a glorified paperweight.

She shoved aside old receipts and something suspiciously sticky before yanking open a drawer. The inhaler sat inside like an old lover waiting for her return. Sleek. Waiting. Shadow's promise curled at the edge of her mind; not relief exactly, more like absence, more like drowning while whispering finally.

Her fingers trembled around it. One second of hesitation. Then none at all as she raised it to her lips. "Come to me, my beauty."

"Talking to yourself again?"

Lori's voice snapped through the haze like a blade between ribs: sharp, knowing, just amused enough to be infuriating. She stood in the doorway watching with that smirk that meant trouble was coming whether or not Marti was ready for it.

"Go to hell," Marti muttered.

Lori stepped inside instead of leaving, which figured. "Maybe later," she said. "But first? We've got a job to do."

Marti let her eyes drift toward the inhaler one last time before tucking it away again; out of sight but never out of reach. "Yeah," she said.

Lori didn't move. She watched her before nodding as if she'd decided something Marti wasn't in on yet. "Good," she said as if they were talking about something else entirely.

She turned on her heel and strode back into the main office without looking back, because Lori never looked back first, and let the door swing shut behind her with finality that didn't stick when Marti fished out the inhaler again and took a hit.

Shadow flooded through her like ink spilling into water, blotting out everything sharp and bright until only weightless black remained.

Chapter 2

Marti's office twisted around her; the walls breathing, the stacks of files sprawling into some nightmarish jungle. Empty coffee cups curled into skeletal branches, stretching for something unseen. The air thickened, damp and cloying, pressing against her skin as if in a fever dream.

"Welcome back," a voice purred in her ear: low, slick, familiar. Smoke curling through her skull. "Miss us?"

Her pulse spiked. "Who's 'us'?" But she knew. She always knew.

A shape prowled through the warped shadows: sleek, silent, predatory. A tiger, its neon-glow eyes locking onto hers, tail flicking against the wreckage of memory piled inside her head. A specter of all her worst mistakes, stalking her as if she deserved it.

"Fuck off," she muttered.

The tiger didn't vanish.

"You need us," the voice pressed on, smooth as whiskey and twice as dangerous. "You need your failures to keep you warm at night." It slithered around her like a snake wrapping tight, tight, tighter. "Without them, who even are you?"

Marti bared her teeth in something that wasn't a smile. "Better."

Laughter skated down her spine like ice water. "There's no 'better' for people like you," the voice crooned. "Just different shades of fucked."

"Get out of my head!" She dug her fingers into her temples as if she could claw the hallucination out by force.

And then it shattered.

She hit the floor hard enough to rattle her teeth, gasping. The world was back: her real world. Coffee-stained files, burned-out neon flickering in from outside, cigarette smoke clinging to every regret. Sweat dripped from her brow; her heart jackhammered in her chest. Her inhaler lay beside her, empty and useless.

"Tainted," she rasped to no one but herself. Fucking hell... that had been a bad one.

The office door creaked open.

Marti snapped up so fast black spots crowded the edges of her vision. The ghost of neon tiger-eyes lurked in the corners of the room, but Lori was there too, real and solid and grounding.

"Hey, boss." Lori leaned against the doorframe with that half-smirk that meant trouble or coffee or both. "You havin' a nice little chat with yourself in here?"

Marti dragged a hand down her face and exhaled through gritted teeth. "Fuck off."

"That bad?"

No point lying about it; not when Lori could see through bullshit like glass anyway.

Marti pulled herself up onto shaky legs and swiped at the sweat on her brow with a shaking hand. "Yeah."

Lori didn't push, which was why Marti hadn't shot her yet, but she didn't drop it either.

"Well," Lori said, "if you're done playing ghost whisperer with your personal demons, we've got work."

The word 'demons' crawled under Marti's skin as if barbed wire tightened around bone, but whatever Lori saw in Marti's face made her smirk widen instead of retreat.

"Missing person case," Lori went on as she stepped inside and dropped a folder onto Marti's desk with a satisfying slap of paper against wood. "Low-level Shadow runner with friends in high places: rich family wants their little fuck-up found." Her grin turned sharp as she tilted her head toward Marti and added, "Thought you might like this one."

Marti stared down at the file without touching it.

She needed another cigarette.

Or another hit.

Or maybe just another minute before diving into more missing pieces nobody would want to find.

Instead, she exhaled and clicked at the folder.

"Yeah," she muttered under her breath as she flipped it open.

"Let's get on with it."

"Money doesn't bring back lost kids, Lori," Marti muttered, flicking ash into the overfilled tray as she skimmed the file.

Lori leaned against the desk, arms crossed, a smirk playing at her lips. "No, but it pays the bills. Unless you wanna start working pro bono?"

Marti snorted. "Since when are you such an optimist?"

"Must be your influence, boss." Lori grinned, dimples deepening. "Now are we taking this case or what?"

Marti snapped the folder shut. "Yeah. Fine."

"Great," Lori said, clapping her hands together. "I'll let them know we're on it. Get everything set up in the system."

She turned to leave, and Marti let her go, but her thoughts churned like sludge through rusted pipes. Same fucking ghosts, same weight pressing down. Failures stacked like bricks against her ribs. Shadow whispered at the edges of her mind, curling in like smoke, promising relief even as it laughed at her restraint. Sobriety wasn't a goddamn victory. It was punishment.

She dragged a hand over her face, swallowing down the itch for something sharper than nicotine.

"Hey, Marti?" Lori's voice from the doorway now, softer than before, as if she knew better than to ask but couldn't help herself. "You good?"

"Fucking paradise." Marti bared a smile that tasted like glass shards.

Lori hesitated for a beat too long, then disappeared down the hall, leaving Marti alone with the case and all the bullshit it dragged behind it.

Marti drummed her fingers against the desk, glaring at the screen as if it had personally wronged her. Missing low-level dealer: Henry Gardner. The folder was already sitting on the server, pristine and waiting, because Lori fucking knew she'd take the job before she even admitted it to herself.

And then it hit.

Gardner.

Her gut turned to ice, recognition hitting like a steel-toed kick to the ribs.

No fucking way.

Henry Gardner, related to Kevin Gardner? The Kevin Gardner? The bastard who ran half of Falls City's drug trade? That piece of shit had a kid?

No goddamn way.

"Lori?"

A beat, then: "What?" Somewhere down the hall, her voice was muffled but sharp.

Marti swallowed against the tightness in her throat. "Kevin Gardner; what the fuck is this?"

"Henry, not Kevin," Lori shot back, as if that was supposed to help.

"And who's footing the bill?"

Silence stretched long enough to confirm what Marti already suspected. Then: "Uh... oh. Kevin? Why... what's the big fucking deal?" Lori stepped into the office, arms folded, expression wary.

Marti flicked a hand at her in dismissal, mostly an excuse to watch her walk away. She shoved aside a mountain of smart-paper pads and real paper pads until she found her phone buried beneath the mess. That she still knew Kevin Gardner's number by heart said far too much about her life choices.

"Starova, for Kevin Gardner," she said as soon as some lackey picked up.

The hold music was excruciating: some tinny piano track that made her want to punch through a wall. But finally, Gardner's voice crawled into her ear like an oil slick. "Starova," he drawled, "what have you got?"

"A bad addiction." She leaned back in her chair and lit a cigarette. "How about you?"

"Your money," he said. "Thanks for the contribution. Found Henry yet?"

Marti exhaled smoke toward the ceiling and reached for a pen. "Just opened the file." She snatched a half-used quickwrite pad off her desk and scrawled his name across the top in jagged letters. "Why are you hiring me for this?"

"You think I can send my men into someone else's turf without starting a fucking war?" His tone held enough condescension to make her want to throw something at his face. "I need to know where my boy is." A beat of silence stretched between them before he added: "Make sure he's okay."

She let that sit for a second before snorting. "Yeah, alright. Whose turf?"

"Thornfield."

"The dead guy."

"His wife is running his business with less than a day of downtime."

"Fast."

"You taking the job?"

Marti exhaled smoke and reached for the whiskey in her desk drawer. "How much did my secretary charge you?"

"Ten crisp."

Marti paused mid-pour and smirked. "It's fifty."

"Fuck off."

"Fifty," she repeated. "I'm gonna have to crawl through a lot of shit to find him; literal shit, probably." She tore off a note from the pad with a satisfying rip: Lori – Gardner $50k. "You know I can go anywhere in this town without causing a war. You want me? You pay."

Gardner sighed loud enough that she could hear it over the line. "Fine, Starova." A wry twist laced his voice now: a dark amusement layered under something harder. "You'll be paying it back soon enough in sales."

He wasn't wrong about that part. "I'll be in touch," she said as she hung up.

Marti grabbed another quickwrite pad and flipped open a search tab on her screen. Time to start digging through garbage, both digital and otherwise.

The flickering holo-tab cast an icy blue glow across her face as she focused on the screen. "Alright, let's do this," she muttered, dragging her finger across the interface to fire up the deep web search engine. With a few taps, she summoned Henry Gardner's name, eyes narrowing as the results populated before her: a mishmash of social media links, public records, scattered forum posts dripping with cryptic hints. None of it felt right; nothing from people who knew him, or at least had anything useful to share.

With a sigh, Marti slammed her fingers on the keyboard and launched into the real work for a private investigator. Venturing into Gardner territory was forbidden, but anywhere else was fair game. Hours evaporated as she navigated the chaotic underbelly of the city, dodging the thrumming pulse of Thornfield's demonized space. The word was out: Marcus Thornfield had taken the big one, and what was left behind was a ripe free-for-all among wannabe overlords desperate to claim his turf.

As long as she could score a hit of cheap Fentafill and Shadow, Marti didn't give a damn. All that mattered was tracking down Henry Gardner, the son of a kingpin who'd want her head on a platter if she fucked this up. The pit in her stomach twisted as she recalled the stakes.

"Seen this guy?" she barked at a blond kid sprinting from a nearby alley, the grainy photo of Gardner clutched in her hand.

To her surprise, the kid stopped, squinted at the picture, and broke into laughter. "I beat you to him!" he shouted before bolting away, leaving her with nothing but frustration racing through her veins.

"Argh!" Marti cursed, her anger bubbling as she rolled her head back and trudged into the alley.

Chaos lay before her as blood streaked down the concrete like a twisted art piece. She slammed her hand on her phone, reminding herself that she wasn't devoid of humanity, and called emergency services.

As she edged closer to the body, relief washed over her. It wasn't Gardner. Close, but not close enough to matter. "Yeah, I'd like to report a body in the alley behind..." she glanced at the door sign, "Gina's Salon: Deliveries Only."

"Gina's Salon. At Limit and Front," she repeated.

A slew of questions followed, the operator sticking to the protocol as if it were lifeblood. "Do you know the person? Are they breathing? Do you know what happened? Can I have your name?"

"Damian Kane," she replied, smirking at the thought. "Tell him I said hi," and she hung up, knowing the jab would rankle him.

Finding dead bodies seemed to have become one of her talents, far exceeding what statistics might suggest was normal. Fuck normal.

She made it a point to notify emergency services every time, always leaving a taunt for Kane, her once-homicide partner. He'd tried to be her rock when she was spiraling downward. Now she was out of that life, still holding onto a thread of connection.

Siren wails pierced the night air as she stepped back from the dead guy, heart racing with a mix of adrenaline and dread. The alley swallowed her up, and she figured the guy had only played the wrong hand in the chaotic game of survival. She knew the stakes too well to linger.

Time to bounce, she told herself, wanting to escape the darkness that lurked behind every corner.

The rain hit the pavement in heavy sheets, each drop fracturing the neon reflections into broken kaleidoscopes of color. Marti pulled her collar higher, though it did little against the chill that had seeped into her bones. Her fingers trembled as she fished the small orange bottle from her pocket, tipping two Fentafill pills into her palm before returning it to its hiding place. Dry swallow. Thirty minutes until the edge softened.

She stepped over a man curled against a storefront, his face hidden under a soaked newspaper. No reaction when her boot splashed too close. Dead or just dead to the world: it didn't matter which in Falls City.

"Henry Gardner, where are you?" she muttered, studying the dog-eared photograph again. The face was imprinted in her memory, but the ritual helped focus her thoughts when they threatened to scatter as if roaches under light.

A police cruiser rolled past, its tires cutting through the ankle-deep puddles. The officer inside didn't look her way. Three buildings down, she spotted him slide a package through a basement window, then drive off with his headlights dark.

Marti turned down Cathode Alley, where the defunct electronics shops had transformed into makeshift pharmacies. The smell hit her first: burned plastic and chemical sweetness. A woman with hollow cheeks offered her a syringe without a word. Marti shook her head, though her veins ached in protest.

"Looking for someone," Marti said, voice rough from disuse. She held up the photo, protected in a clear sleeve smudged with fingerprints. "Seen him?"

The woman's pupils contracted to pinpoints under the harsh light of a nearby vending machine. Recognition flickered before vanishing. "Haven't seen him," she said, but her eyes darted toward the corner building with boards over the windows and a red door that hung ajar.

Marti slipped her a few crumpled bills anyway. Information had a price in Falls City, even the unspoken kind.

The pills were starting to work now, smoothing the jagged edges of her perception. She could feel her hands steadying, her mind sharpening into something almost functional. Six hours before she'd need another dose. Six hours to find Henry before withdrawal pulled her under again.

She approached the red door, water streaming from her hair down her neck. The security camera above was a gutted shell, wires dangling as if entrails. Someone had spray-painted an eye over the lens: the ubiquitous tag of the Watchers syndicate, the cartel that owned these two square blocks.

Marti's stomach tightened. If Henry had gotten mixed up with them, if they found out who he was, she might only find pieces of him.

As she reached for the door, her reflection caught in a puddle: gaunt face, dark circles, eyes that couldn't decide between desperate or determined. Falls City had a way of making everyone look as if they were drowning, even when they stood on solid ground.

Marti pushed the door open, and darkness said hello.

It gave way to strobing light: a busted fluorescent panel that couldn't decide between life and death. The hallway stretched before her, walls tattooed with graffiti, floor sticky with substances Marti chose not to identify. She moved forward, listening to muted voices filtering through paper-thin walls.

Room after room revealed nothing but the usual Falls City tableau: junkies lost in chemical dreams, mumbling incoherencies to ghosts only they could see. No Henry Gardner.

At the end of the hall, a mountain of a man stood guard before a steel door. His neck was a canvas of prison ink, stories of violence etched in blue-black lines. Marti approached, photo extended like an offering.

"Looking," she said. The man's expression remained blank, but his eyes flickered with recognition before hardening again. "Need to talk to him. It's about his sister."

A lie, but family still meant something in Falls City. One of the few things that did.

"Not here," the man rumbled, but his gaze shifted to the floor, a tell Marti had learned to recognize years ago.

"His sister's dying," Marti pressed, letting her voice crack. "Cancer. Wants to see him before she goes."

The guard's jaw worked in silence, conscience and orders battling behind his eyes. He leaned closer, breath hot against her ear. "Try the old boat factory. Third floor. But you didn't hear it from me."

Marti slipped him a twenty: a gesture of respect that would keep his mouth shut if anyone asked. As she turned to leave, his meaty hand caught her shoulder.

"You be careful," he said, something like concern in his voice.

Did she know him? Or did her reputation precede her? Marti didn't answer. Didn't need to.

"You go in soft or don't come out at all."

Outside, the rain had stopped, leaving the streets slick and gleaming under the sickly glow of sodium lights. Marti checked her watch: 4:28 AM. The pills were holding, but an itch was beginning to crawl beneath her skin.

The boat factory stood like a monolith at the edge of the industrial district, as if from when Falls City manufactured something other than misery. Every window had been smashed years ago, leaving dark sockets that watched her approach.

She made it as far as the loading dock before the dizzy spell hit. The world tilted sideways, her vision tunneling to a pinpoint. Not withdrawal; something else. The memory surfaced: the woman in the alley, brushing too close as she pointed toward the red door. A needle, perhaps. Or something in the air at the flophouse. Or in the bouncer's touch.

Fuck.

Drugged. Amateur mistake.

Marti braced herself against a wall, fighting to stay conscious. Her gun felt heavy in its holster. In her condition, she'd be dead before she cleared leather.

"Damn it," she muttered, staggering back toward the street.

The journey back was a blur of half-remembered streets and near falls. Twice she had to hide from police cruisers, though whether they were legitimate or just thugs in stolen uniforms, she couldn't tell.

Dawn was breaking by the time she fumbled with the keys to her office. The peeling letters on the frosted glass door read "M RTI ST VA INVE TIGATI NS": the missing letters never replaced, like teeth knocked out in a fight.

Inside smelled of stale coffee and relief. She collapsed onto the ancient leather couch against the wall, springs groaning in protest beneath her weight.

As consciousness began to slip away, Marti's fingers closed around the orange pill bottle in her pocket. She'd need it. Some time.

In Falls City, everyone was lost.

Her eyes closed, and for a few hours, she joined the ranks of those who escaped the city the only way they could: through dreams or drugs or death. In Marti's case, it was hard to tell the difference anymore.

Another night had bled away before she found herself still sitting there, unmoved except for a fresh pile of cigarette butts smoldering in their grave beside her coffee cup long gone cold. The neon glow outside flickered against rain-slick pavement, painting shadows across her walls in restless, shifting shapes she couldn't quite look at directly.

The sun crept up like an uninvited guest before Marti realized how much time had passed. Fuck it. Sleep had never done her any favors anyway.

It was a rough night.

Footsteps approached from down the hall before Lori pushed open the door with a steaming cup in hand, shaking it until Marti looked up to acknowledge its existence.

"Brought you coffee," Lori said as she stepped inside, setting it down within reach before dropping onto the edge of Marti's desk as if she belonged there, which maybe she did by now. "Not great coffee, but functional enough to keep your ass upright."

Marti took it without protest and wrapped cold fingers around its heat. "I need function more than quality right now."

She stared at Lori through the steam, letting her mind wander along hemlines and cleavage.

Lori smirked over her own cup before taking a slow sip and watching her over the rim. "Yeah," she said after an unreadable pause. "Figured."

"What have you got for me?" Lori asked, stretching out over Marti's desk as if she was settling in for a long day. "Tell me we've got something on Henry and not just another dead end."

Marti flipped open her notebook. She had, against all odds, done some actual work.

"Jack shit so far," she said, dragging a finger through the dust collecting along the desk's edge. "But word on the street says there's a Fentafill shipment incoming. Big one. And since Henry's a runner, well." She shrugged. "Could be he's tied up in it."

Lori exhaled, rubbing her temples as if she could smooth out the headache forming between them. "Great. Just what this city needs: more overdoses, more bodies, more fuckups who don't know when to quit." Her eyes flicked back to Marti's, sharp now instead of tired. "Did your sources give you anything useful? Location? Timing?"

"If by 'useful' you mean vague half-truths and drunken speculation, then yeah, plenty." Marti leaned back and crossed her arms. "Nothing concrete yet. But someone always slips up when there's product moving. We'll find the trail." Her voice came out steady, but her stomach twisted at the thought of chasing down the very thing she'd been trying to outrun for years. "And we'll find Henry. Did you charge Gardner the 50 crisp?"

"Yeah," Lori said, jaw tight. "No fucking doubt about it."

"Good. I had to put up with some shit last night. Something's up."

"With Kevin? Henry?" Lori asked, raising an eyebrow.

"No, neither. I mean, the streets are shifting. Someone drugged me last night," Marti said, lighting a cigarette and taking a long drag.

"Without your permission?" Lori smirked, leaning back in her chair.

"Yes. Asshole. I don't know exactly what or when, but I found a body in an alley and."

"You what?" Lori shouted, her eyes wide.

"Yeah, a body. Someone put a price on some kid's head. He looked like a nothing. I called it in. But then I got spiked. If I wasn't so used to functioning in a fog, I could be dead."

Lori's expression softened, tears threatening to spill.

Marti blew a stream of smoke towards the ceiling, her eyes scanning the chaos of her office: files stacked carelessly, quickwrite notes hanging by a thread, empty Shadow inhalers scattered like forgotten promises. "Might as well see if any of my mess is useful."

Great transition, Starova.

Lori rolled her eyes but didn't argue, reaching for a stack of papers with all the enthusiasm of someone digging through trash for treasure.

They worked in relative silence, sifting through scrawls and photos Marti took with her phone. The room smelled like whiskey and stale cigarettes, an oppressive mix of exhaustion and Marti's unwashed clothes that neither one of them commented on.

"Here," Lori said, rustling paper breaking the quiet. She tugged a crumpled note free from beneath a pile of half-forgotten intel and held it up. "This is from when I first started looking into Fentafill; it's got names on it. People who were dealing back then." She glanced at Marti. "Could be one of them is still in business. Might know where Henry is?"

Marti plucked the note from Lori's fingers and scanned it, eyes narrowing as she read each name. "Yeah," she murmured. "This is something we can use."

"Fuck yeah, it is." Lori grinned before schooling her expression into something more professional. Marti caught the flash of pride in her face.

Marti smirked but didn't call her on it. Her fingers twitched toward her desk, toward the sleek inhaler lying there like an unanswered question. The metallic gleam caught the dim light, whispering promises she wasn't stupid enough to believe anymore but still wanted to anyway.

Her throat went dry as she dragged herself away from it, standing and wandering toward the window. Outside, neon spilled across wet pavement in garish colors, too bright, too fake, painting everything in shades of sin and consequence. The city pulsed below her as if it were an open wound no one could stitch shut long enough to heal.

She shifted her focus to Lori, reflected in the glass. Could anything dull that woman's shine?

She pressed her fingertips against the glass. Cold bit at her skin; clarity followed close behind.

Behind her, Lori shifted but didn't speak, just watched, as if she knew exactly what kind of war was happening inside Marti's head but wouldn't push unless necessary.

Marti exhaled, fogging up part of the window before wiping it clean with her sleeve as if that would fix anything.

"Let's get to work," she said.

Lori didn't hesitate.

"Thought you'd never ask." She left the room, taking that sweet ass with her.

Marti had time to pour herself another whiskey before Lori rolled back in like she was the Prohibition police, booting the door shut behind her.

"A rat bastard is here to hire you," she announced, as if this was supposed to be good news.

Marti blinked at her. "Be more specific."

"You'll see."

The door swung open before Marti could throw anything at Lori for being cryptic.

Ari Stirling stepped in like he belonged there, polished shoes clicking against the linoleum with deliberation to make it clear he wanted people watching. He moved like a man used to getting what he wanted; he usually did.

"Martina Starova." His voice had that rich, oiled quality some men cultivated when they thought charm doubled as currency. "A pleasure."

She didn't stand. Just took a long sip of whiskey and leveled him with a look over the rim of her mug. "We'll see about that."

Stirling smiled, all teeth, and dropped into the chair across from her desk without waiting for an invitation. His fitted suit hardly creased when he moved. That kind of fabric cost money, real money: the kind that bought silence and influence in equal measure. The kind Marcus Thornfield and his people liked to throw around.

Which begged the question: why the hell was one of Thornfield's protégés sitting in Marti's office?

"Mr. Stirling," she said, setting her mug aside with a clink against the wood. "To what do I owe the dubious honor?"

"Please," he said, brushing lint from his sleeve. "Call me Ari."

"No."

Lori snorted from where she'd parked herself against the filing cabinet, arms folded across her chest as if she was enjoying the show. Stirling ignored her, too busy playing whatever game he thought this was with Marti. His dark eyes locked on hers as if they were circling each other in some metaphorical ring only he could see.

"I've heard quite a bit about you," he said, head tilting as if studying a specimen under glass. "Your skills. Your reputation." He let that last word hang like bait, waiting for her to bite.

She didn't. Just arched an brow and drummed her fingers against her desk. "Cut to the part where I give a shit."

Stirling huffed and reached into his jacket with care, no tension in his shoulders, no tells, as if he wanted it noted that reaching inside his coat wasn't something anyone needed to worry about yet. From an inner pocket, he withdrew a photograph and slid it across the desk with all the ceremony of a poker player tossing out chips.

Marti didn't pick it up right away. She let her gaze flick down as it landed in front of her, absorbing what she already knew before she made a show of looking at it properly.

Marcus Thornfield smirked up at her from glossy paper, all precision-cut hair and porcelain teeth: the kind of man who could trade pleasantries at charity galas while laundering money through half the city's underground network without breaking stride. His eyes were cold despite his smile. They always had been.

Stirling leaned back in his chair, watching for her reaction; she didn't give him much to work with beyond picking up the photo and flicking it between two fingers like it meant nothing at all.

"Everyone knows Marcus Thornfield. And that he offed himself just the other day," she said, tossing it back onto the desk between them. "You're going to have to try harder if you want my attention."

"One hundred crisp."

"You have my attention."

"Marcus is dead," Stirling said, watching her like a cat watches a twitching mouse. "Five days ago. Official report says suicide." A pause. Then, with amusement: "But I have my doubts. He'd never ruin that perfect face with a bullet."

Marti snorted, tapping ash into the closest empty mug. "You want me to weep for him? Light a candle and cry into my whiskey?" She shook her head. "Men like Thornfield are a plague. They burn bright, crash hard, leave wreckage wherever they land."

Stirling inclined his head, conceding the point. "Oh please. Politicians and priests are the real plague. But his death stinks, and I think you're the only one who can find out why."

She drummed two fingers against the desk: tap, tap, tap. The tempo of uncertainty settled in her ribs. A criminal empire shouldn't need her for this kind of thing; they had their own muscle, their own fixers. Yet here Stirling was, making it sound like she was his only option.

Like Gardner.

Something about it gnawed at her instincts, as if it were a locked door she didn't have a key for. Everything in her said to walk away. But then again, she had nothing better to do than get lost in another miserable case.

"Marti," Stirling murmured, leaning forward so his elbows hit the desk, voice low and coaxing. "I need someone with your expertise." His lips curved like he knew what she'd say next.

She leaned back instead of forward, arms crossing over her ribs as if to guard her from whatever bullshit he was selling. "And when you say 'expertise,' you mean…?"

Ari's smirk was like nicotine through the lungs: pure satisfaction. "Your reputation precedes you. A Shadow addict who knows every alley and backroom in this city. Someone with friends in every part of Falls City. And no connections to any other corporation, if you will. You're exactly who I need."

She exhaled like she could clear him out of her system with sheer force of will. "Look," she said, leveling him with a glance sharp enough to cut glass, "I don't love cops any more than you do, but I don't see why you'd come to me instead of them. What's your angle here?"

Ari's smirk didn't waver. It edged sharper. "The cops closed the case. Here's the file."

Marti waved him off, but Lori reached out to take the envelope. She pulled out less than a dozen sheets.

"You'll find everything they did. Verified alibis, interviewed nobodies, got nowhere," Stirling said. "Called it suicide and washed their hands clean before the ink on the report dried. But it was murder." His eyes gleamed in the dim light as he tilted his head toward her, voice dropping lower. "And if there's one thing I know about you? You're good at catching murderers."

Marti huffed out a laugh with no humor in it. "Flattery's cute, but my days with Falls City PD are long past," she said, though something dark and restless coiled under her skin. This was what she used to be good at: untangling shit no one else wanted to touch. She felt its pull now like an old habit trying to worm its way home again.

"Fine," she sighed after another beat of silence, fingers tapping once before going still. "What have you got?"

Stirling sat back in his chair like he had her answer from the start. The rat bastard was right. He steepled his fingers under his chin.

"Marcus was found in his pool house five days ago," he said. "Gunshot wound to the head." He paused before adding: "No gun at the scene."

"His wife was where?"

"Evelyn was in Paris. A copy of her plane ticket is in the file. The maids were out at the movies."

"Security detail?"

"Marcus had none when he was meeting clients."

"Meeting clients?" Marti asked, interested. "In the pool house?"

"His business dealings went to shit recently," Stirling said, his voice dipping into something that might have passed for sympathy if Marti didn't know better. "And when that happens, people get desperate. Marcus was mixed up in some things that made him enemies."

"Oh, for fuck's sake, just say it," Marti drawled, kicking her boots up onto the desk. "Money laundering? Drugs? Arms dealing? Pick your poison. We both know Thornfield wasn't running a charity for orphaned hedge fund managers."

Ari's smirk barely twitched. "Among other things. But he was running a side hustle: blackmail. Not sure what secrets he was gathering. That wasn't corporate business." He exhaled as if savoring the weight of his own words. "I would have known."

Marti gave a low whistle and turned to Lori. "You buying any of this?"

Lori didn't look up from her nails. "I think he's playing you," she said, inspecting the edge of her thumb as if it held the secrets of the universe. "But hey, it's your life."

"And your paycheck," Marti shot back with a grin before turning back to Ari. "Alright, I'll take the case. Lori will send over a contract. One hundred grand."

Stirling stood, satisfaction oozing off him in waves: expensive cologne and moneyed arrogance wrapped up in a bespoke suit. "I knew you wouldn't disappoint."

Marti took a drag off her cigarette, letting the smoke curl between them before exhaling straight toward his retreating form. "Oh, I absolutely will," she said. "Just depends on who you ask."

Stirling reached the door and hesitated just long enough to turn back and murmur, "Call me first when you figure it out." Then he was gone.

Marti leaned back in her chair as the scent of cigarette smoke hung in the air. She exhaled and let herself sit in it, this moment, this feeling, because for the first time in years, something sharpened behind her ribs like a blade catching light. No more half-assed jobs or chasing dead leads for rent money. This was murder; the kind that tangled deep and didn't let go, and fuck if she wasn't already sunk in it past saving.

Lori tapped a pen against the desk, watching her with something unreadable behind those dark eyes of hers. Shadows from the overhead light shifted against her cheekbones like smoke curling away from flame.

"And the missing Henry?" Lori asked.

"We shove him to the back burner," Marti said, running a hand through her hair before reaching for what was left of her coffee. It was cold; she drank it anyway. It had no butts in it.

Lori hummed in her throat and stretched in her chair, long legs crossing at the ankle as she considered it.

Oh, those ankles.

"Thornfield had layers," she mused, her voice dipping into something almost hypnotic. "How do we peel them back? He must have had as many secrets as side pieces."

Marti snorted and stubbed out what was left of her cigarette in an overflowing ashtray. "Don't they all?"

She felt the itch then, the craving crawling under her skin like an old lover whispering come back. She clenched her jaw against it. The last thing she needed was Shadow muddying up an already tangled mess.

"Thornfield wasn't just another rich bastard playing kingpin," she said, her voice rough but steady enough to hold its ground against everything clawing at the edges of her mind. "He knew how to wield power, how to twist people so tight they walked themselves right into their own graves without realizing he'd been pulling the strings."

She dragged a hand through her hair before meeting Lori's eyes.

"Drugs, sex, crime: you name it," Marti murmured. "Thornfield had his fingers in every pie."

And now? Those fingers were cold as marble, and someone out there was real fucking happy about that.

Time to find out why.

"Why the hell would Stirling come to us?" Lori asked, arms crossed, expression flat. "Did the cops suddenly forget how to do their jobs?"

Marti exhaled. "You heard him. They won't touch it. Written off as a suicide. Case closed." She flicked at a peeling edge of the label on her coffee cup, voice tight. "No gun at the scene, and they still shut it down? Bullshit."

Lori watched her, eyes narrowed. "Or maybe you just want to fuck with Homicide for kicking you out."

Marti held her gaze, steady as a loaded gun. Then she shrugged. "Maybe. Not like I'm the only one who wants the truth for all the wrong reasons."

Lori snorted. "Or to bury it." Her tone was unreadable, but something twisted beneath it: distrust, curiosity, something else Marti didn't have time to name. She leaned back in her chair and turned toward her desk as if this was just another job. Maybe for her, it was.

Marti dragged a cigarette from her pocket and rolled it between her fingers without lighting it. Fucking Shadow had rewired her brain; one addiction bleeding into another. She'd take withdrawal over looking weak in front of Lori any day.

"Thanks for the vote of confidence," she said, gaze flicking to the photo of Thornfield on her desk. His smile was pure smug bastard, as if he knew he'd left one last trail of wreckage behind just for an asshole like her to pick through.

The room settled into silence except for the hum of the neon sign outside casting red light across the floorboards. She stared at Thornfield's face and felt old ghosts pressing in from all sides: failures, bad calls, regrets curling tight around her ribs like barbed wire.

"Suicide, my ass," she muttered.

Chapter 3

The office smelled like old cigarettes and regrets. Marti slumped into her chair, rubbing at the tension in her neck, but it didn't help. Nothing did lately. The air was thick, stale, pressing in as if the walls were closing. Maybe they were. Maybe she'd lost it.

Her eyes dragged to the corkboard on the far wall, where Marcus Thornfield's face stared back at her in grainy black and white. Even dead, the bastard had a presence: sharp jaw, broad shoulders, that look as if he knew every dirty secret she had. He probably did. He was the reason Shadow existed, after all. And Shadow had owned her for a long time.

Her desk groaned as she leaned forward, a headache pulsed at her temples. There it sat right in front of her like a goddamn invitation: the inhaler. Small, silver, harmless-looking if you didn't know better. Harmless until it wasn't.

Her fingers twitched toward it before she could stop herself. Just one hit wouldn't kill her. Wouldn't mean anything. Just enough to take the edge off.

"You're thinking about it."

Marti jerked back like she'd been burned, knocking over a coffee cup in the process. "Fucking hell, Lori."

Lori leaned against the doorway, arms crossed, unimpressed as always. "You jump like that when you're guilty."

Marti shoved the inhaler into the desk drawer and shut it hard. "You spying on me now?"

Lori snorted. "Please. If I were spying on you, I'd be better at it." Her gaze flicked to the corkboard and back as if she'd done this dance before. "So? What have you got on Thornfield?"

"Me? What the fuck have you got?" Marti snorted as she turned on the holo-tab. Thornfield's face shimmered into view.

Marti stabbed Thornfield's face with two fingers before grabbing another cigarette from the pack on her desk. She lit up and inhaled deep enough to burn away whatever craving lingered in her gut. "Someone wanted him gone."

"And you're going to figure out who."

"Right again," Marti said, exhaling smoke toward the ceiling.

Lori pushed off the doorframe and walked over, resting a hip against the desk as she studied Marti. "You sure about this?"

"What kind of question is that?"

"The kind I ask when I see you staring at shit you shouldn't be touching."

Marti crushed out her cigarette and stood up fast enough to make the chair scrape against the floorboards. "Doesn't matter what I want," she said. "Thornfield's death is bullshit, and I'm not letting Homicide piss away a case just because it's easier."

Lori didn't move out of her way; she just watched her with that mix of patience and concern that made Marti want to shove or kiss or ignore her entirely, depending on how her mood was that day. "And if digging into this drags up everything you've been trying to bury?" Lori asked.

Marti held her gaze for half a second before turning away first: coward.

"Then I guess we'll see what crawls out."

Lori walked out and never saw Marti's hand knock against the inhaler as she reached for her mouse. The cold metal a slap against her skin. It sent a shiver up her spine: anticipation, dread, craving.

"Fuck off," she muttered, shoving it away as if that would be enough to quiet the itch crawling through her veins. But it never was. Not really. Shadow never left; it just lingered in the corners of her mind, waiting for her to slip.

The inhale, the rush, the bliss. It would all be so easy. One hit and she wouldn't have to think about this case or Lori's worried eyes or whether she was already in over her head.

Marti flexed her fingers and rolled her shoulders back, shaking off the thought like a bad dream. She wasn't doing this today.

She grabbed the inhaler and slammed it into a drawer with enough force to rattle the desk. Small fucking victory, but she'd take what she could get.

"Time to work," she told herself, reaching for the thin stack of documents Lori had managed to pull together on Thornfield's murder. The facts were shit. The leads were worse. Still, better than nothing, except not by much.

The door creaked open an hour after she buried herself in data, and Lori's voice cut through the silence. "You good?"

Marti exhaled before looking up. "Busy."

Lori stepped inside, arms crossed, green eyes sharp enough to pick apart every one of Marti's bullshit defenses. "Shadow or Thornfield?"

A hollow laugh scraped its way out of Marti's throat as she twirled a pen between her fingers. "Both." She leaned back in her chair, gaze flicking over the scant evidence laid out across the desk as if she might see something new if she squinted hard enough. "This case: it's bigger than anything I've handled since leaving the force."

"And you're afraid you'll fuck it up," Lori said as if it wasn't a question.

Marti snorted and tipped her chin up to meet Lori's gaze. "I don't do fear."

Lori arched a brow but didn't argue; they both knew that was bullshit. Instead, she perched on the edge of the desk like she belonged there and tilted her head, watching Marti with something close to admiration.

"Think about it," Marti said. "If we don't take this case, who will? Cops won't touch it without an incentive package big enough to buy their silence after. Maybe the other PIs in this town are too scared or too incompetent."

She huffed and tapped a finger against Thornfield's file as if that might give them more options than they had here. It wouldn't, but hell if that ever stopped her from trying before.

"Fine," she muttered. "Let's burn this whole thing down."

"The whole fucking thing?" Marti echoed, the words heavier than intended. She hesitated. Just for a second. Long enough to consider telling Lori to get out while she still could. But when she looked at her, at bright eyes burning with something reckless and unwavering, she knew it was pointless. Lori wasn't going anywhere.

"Alright," Marti said. "And if shit goes sideways, you run."

Lori smirked as if that was the funniest thing she'd ever heard. "Yeah, sure," she said. "Not happening."

Marti sighed and took a long drag of her cigarette. Maybe Thornfield's ghost would come back and haunt them both just to save her the headache of arguing with Lori about self-preservation.

"Let's get to work," Lori said, grabbing the file again as if it held all the answers they needed. They weren't about to wade waist-deep into some serious fucking trouble. "I've got a feeling this is going to be one hell of a ride."

Marti didn't answer, just stared at the papers in front of her, fingers tracing the edges of Thornfield's photograph. She felt it then: the pull of the case locking her in place, dragging her further into its orbit like an inevitable goddamn black hole.

Lori leaned back against the desk and exhaled. "I'll dig up everything I can on Thornfield's operations; see who had a reason to put him in the ground." She tapped the page twice, expression unreadable. "Meanwhile, you put out some feelers. Someone knows more than they're saying."

"Yes, boss." Marti snorted at her own joke. She flipped over one of the pages in the file, exposing another photo beneath it: a lab setup, sterile except for the vials lined up on a steel table, each one brimming with something dark and electric in its potential destruction.

"His life's work," she muttered, words bitter as ash on her tongue. "The drug that brought me to my knees."

Lori snorted and tossed her phone onto the desk before leaning closer with a grin. "Who's getting on her knees?"

"Kneeling isn't the problem," Marti mused, rolling a cigarette between her fingers without lighting it. Her mind turned over possibilities faster than she wanted them to. "It's the falling on your face that fucks you up."

Lori watched her for a beat before saying, "Then don't fall." Simple as breathing. Her voice was sharp in that way Marti had learned meant don't argue with me unless you want to lose. "You're stronger than you think," Lori added when Marti still didn't look at her. "You've been through harder."

And maybe that was true, but hard didn't stop being harder. It just wore different faces every time it came back around for another swing at you.

Marti didn't respond. She turned away and pressed a palm flat against Thornfield's file as if she could cut through all the noise in her head and focus on what mattered: tracking down whoever had done this before they decided to clean up loose ends by digging too deep to be found.

Except fuck, the noise wasn't stopping tonight. The familiar ache had started creeping into her bones, settling behind her ribs like an old lover sliding back into bed beside her after too much time apart.

Shadow whispered from where it sat inside her desk drawer: a quiet promise wrapped in slick temptation. Marti clenched her jaw so tight it hurt.

"Give me a minute," she said, voice rough.

Lori studied her for a second before nodding and slipping out without argument. That was worse somehow because Lori knew.

Alone now, Marti raked both hands through her messy hair and let out a breath that did nothing to steady her shaking fingers.

"Damn you," she muttered under her breath, too soft for anyone but herself and whatever ghosts still clung to this office to hear. Not that Shadow gave a shit about curses or regrets or twelve-step programs whispered between cigarette drags at two in the morning when sleep wasn't an option.

Her hand found the inhaler before she could talk herself out of it again; not that she tried this time. She pressed it against parted lips with desperation masquerading as control.

One hit deep into waiting lungs and warmth flooded through every nerve ending as if fire licked along dry paper edges: fast and ravenous and relief even though she knew better by now, knew exactly how temporary this bought peace would be before hunger clawed back twice as vicious as before. But still...

Still, Marti let herself inhale again anyway.

For a few seconds, everything disappeared: no past, no future, just color and sensation swallowing her whole. A head rush of weightlessness, euphoria wrapping tight around her ribs like a lover who never planned to let go. This was why she kept coming back.

The high hit like a freight train. Shadow curled through her veins, whispering sweet nothings in the language of oblivion. Reality split, memories bleeding into hallucinations until nothing felt solid: just a mess of light and noise, tangled up in the promise of forgetting.

But Shadow was an asshole. Like every other bastard in her life, it never stuck around long enough.

The crash came hard and fast. Marti groaned as the weight of the world slammed back down, leaving her slumped over her desk, drenched in sweat, staring at Thornfield's smug face smirking from a photograph she could barely remember pulling out.

"Fuck," she rasped, throat raw. "I can't keep doing this."

"Jesus Christ, Marti." Lori's voice sliced through the static filling her skull: sharp, immediate, pissed as hell. "Get it together."

Marti blinked toward the doorway, where Lori stood with arms crossed and eyes narrowed as if she was debating whether to smack the stupid out of her boss or just walk away. The latter would probably be smarter.

Lori didn't do smart when it came to Marti.

Marti sat up too fast. Her head retaliated. Static roared behind her eyes while the clock on the wall ticked out a taunting reminder: Time lost. Time wasted.

"Spare me the lecture," Marti muttered, wiping at her face with trembling fingers that betrayed how deep Shadow had sunk its claws this time.

"No lecture," Lori said. "Just facts." She leaned against the desk, casual only on the surface. "We've got a body and a suspect moving further out of reach by the second. And you're here getting high instead of solving this shit."

A familiar guilt twisted in Marti's gut; not enough to make her apologize but just enough to sting when she forced herself to meet Lori's gaze again. That look cut deeper than any withdrawal ever had. Disappointment tempered with something worse: worry she hadn't earned but still clung to like a lifeline anyway.

"We can still catch up," Marti said instead, because anything else would stick too hard in her throat alongside regret and self-loathing and all the other lovely things she liked to ignore on principle these days.

Lori scoffed but didn't argue, which meant they were both lying to themselves now. "Then we'd better get moving before you spiral back into whatever bullshit existential crisis you were having before I got here."

Marti smirked despite herself (or maybe because of herself; hard to tell these days) and pushed up from her chair with all the grace of a newborn foal on too much caffeine and too little sleep. "Where're we starting?"

"Public records," Lori said, pulling up files on her tablet because someone actually did their job around here while Marti was busy snorting bad decisions off rock bottom's floorboards.

Right: Thornfield's empire wasn't built on petty crime or sloppy mistakes. It ran smoother than half the legal businesses in Falls City because he understood two simple things: location and demand.

His companies looked clean enough on paper, fast food places scattered across town like pinpricks on a map of predictable misery, but reality told a different story. Cash-heavy operations planted near schools for hopeful kids who'd never get their shot. Strip clubs for men trying to forget how much they hated their lives. Suburbia for housewives numbing themselves between PTA meetings and boring husbands who never noticed where their money went after dark.

Overdose reports stacked higher near his locations than anywhere else in Falls City, but here was the strange part: no drug busts at his places for years now despite escalating raids everywhere else in town except his stores. This meant either Thornfield had luck that made Vegas jealous or cops who knew exactly which pockets they were supposed to stay tucked inside of when shit went sideways.

Neither option made catching his killer easier; nothing ever did.

"Alright," Marti said, rolling stiffness from her shoulders and stepping into whatever came next as if she hadn't been one hit away from unconsciousness five minutes ago. "Let's ruin some guy's life."

Lori nodded once, sharp and certain, and grabbed her coat without another word before heading for the door as if she already knew Marti would follow without needing confirmation first.

She wasn't wrong.

Marti lit a cigarette with shaking hands and exhaled slow before trailing after her into whatever fresh hell waited outside that office door.

At least this time she was sober enough to appreciate it. For now.

Hours blurred together, turning into days as they chased leads that crumbled in their hands the second they tightened their grip. Thornfield's ghost clung to Falls City like cigarette smoke in cheap motel curtains: impossible to scrub out, no matter how hard you tried.

They found shell corporations with enough layers to make an onion jealous. A transportation company, three bars, two strip joints; all part of the portfolio. Digital broadsheets whispered about bribes at the docks and City Hall, but nothing stuck. Nothing ever did when men with money were involved.

Marti's gut twisted, an old hunger gnawing at her ribs. Money. Answers. Maybe just something to do with her hands other than reaching for another hit of Shadow. She clenched her fists, flexed them open again. The withdrawal was manageable for now, but Lori's presence was the only thing keeping her from drowning in it. Not that she'd say that out loud.

The phone dinged.

Marti glanced at the screen before answering her phone. "Yeah?"

"Got your request pushed through," said a bored voice on the other end. "Estate transfer was finalized this morning. Evelyn Delacroix inherits everything."

Marti leaned back in her chair, twirling a pen between her fingers. "Appreciate it. That rush fee covering the paperwork too, or just your coffee habit?"

"After the wire transfer clears, you'll have the documents in an hour."

She smirked. "Pleasure doing business."

Hanging up, she clicked open her banking app. A few keystrokes later, the bribe (sorry, rush service fee) was on its way.

"Thornfield's widow hit the jackpot," Marti muttered loudly enough to prick Lori's ears, because who didn't love to prick the woman's ears? "Maybe big enough to get him killed."

Lori hustled in, leaning against the desk, brow furrowed in thought. "Everything to only her? What does that come to? Half a billion?"

Marti scratched her head, trying not to look at Lori's soft skin as she leaned close. She let her eyes travel, her mind wander, and her legs squeeze together.

"Hey, stupid. Pay attention."

Marti let out a slow breath, flicking ash into an overflowing tray. "Did you just call me stupid?" Her lips curled at the edges, but there wasn't any real anger behind it. Of course she was stupid; anyone who let themselves be lead around by that part of their body was going to be distracted.

"An expose on Thornfield last year put him at three quarters of a billion," Marti said. "That's motive, means and opportunity all in one. This is going to be easy."

Except easy was never how this shit worked, not in Falls City. Lights stretched across the office walls as if they had something to say about it, as if they recognized something familiar in her, as if they knew her darkness better than she did herself.

Chapter 4

"You sure this isn't stupid?" Lori asked as they stood outside Evelyn Delacroix's house: three stories of wealth and no morals glaring down at them like a rich aunt who judged your entire existence on sight alone.

"There's that word again," Marti said as she lit a cigarette.

The mansion had been beautiful once, before time and neglect sank their teeth into it and refused to let go. A lot of old houses in the Jefferson Knolls neighborhood were like that. Sandstone walls bore weather scars; dying ivy clung on for dear life as if it knew once it let go, there was no coming back from that fall. The wrought-iron gates groaned when Marti pushed them open, resisting as if even they thought this was a bad idea.

Stone gargoyles flanked the entrance: ugly bastards, grimacing as if they'd seen every sin ever committed inside and weren't impressed by a single one. Heavy drapes smothered every window, hiding whatever lurked behind them from curious eyes.

Is it really this easy to get this close to a widow worth almost a billion?

Marti took another drag off her cigarette and exhaled before grinding it under her heel on the cobblestone driveway.

"This is probably a terrible idea," she admitted.

Then she knocked anyway.

Evelyn Delacroix answered the door as if she was stepping onto a stage: poised, perfect, and barely holding it together. Her black silk dress clung to her like grief itself, raven hair spilling over her shoulders in a way that seemed practiced. The widow costume suited her.

Her eyes flicked between Marti and Lori, sapphire-hard but rimmed red, with a look that said she wasn't as untouched by tragedy as she wanted people to think. "You're not reporters," she said, voice smooth as poured whiskey but threaded with something darker underneath.

Marti didn't smile. "Ari Stirling hired us," she said. "Wants us to look into your husband's death."

Something tightened in Evelyn's jaw, a barely-there recoil, before she smoothed it out with a slow blink. Then she stepped aside, granting them entry with a nod that felt more like surrender than hospitality.

Inside, the Delacroix mansion was all cavernous halls and ghost-heavy silence. It smelled expensive: old wood, lingering perfume, wealth baked into every surface. Shadows stretched beneath chandeliers that spilled light but not warmth.

"Pauline," Evelyn called, voice carrying through the house as if it belonged there.

A moment later, Pauline appeared: not rushed, not hesitant, just there, moving as if she knew she was being watched and didn't mind.

Marti held back a smirk. Well, shit.

The maid was exactly as Marti remembered: dark-eyed and full-lipped, her body curved in ways that had once left Marti breathless against unfamiliar sheets. Back then, Pauline had whispered something against her throat (French? Or maybe just nonsense meant to sound pretty) and Marti had been too drunk on sex to care which it was.

She had no idea Pauline was Evelyn's or Marcus's maid, but she might be a vital source of information. Or something.

"I'm Lori Harring. This is..."

Those lips curled into the ghost of a smirk. "Marti," Pauline murmured, tilting her head just enough to let her hair spill forward over one shoulder. "Marti Starova. I thought you looked familiar."

Lori and Evelyn were already heading toward the living room, leaving them alone in thickening silence. Pauline took a step closer: not touching yet, but close enough for Marti to feel heat rolling off her skin in waves.

"It's been a while," Marti muttered.

Pauline made a soft sound in response, almost a laugh, and reached out to toy with the lapel of Marti's jacket. "And yet here we are."

There were plenty of reasons this was a bad idea. Potential suspects shouldn't be fingered in both senses of the word. Widows tended to frown on their maids getting fucked against their kitchen counters. Marti had work to do that did not involve chasing old indulgences down dark hallways. But Pauline smelled just as warm and sinful as before, and logic had never been one of Marti's strong suits anyway.

Pauline shifted closer; Marti caught the scent of something floral clinging to her wrist before she tilted her chin up in invitation, eyes flashing under long lashes.

So much for restraint.

Marti pressed Pauline back against the nearest wall with deliberation, hands sliding up beneath stiff fabric until fingertips met skin: soft and waiting and warm with want. She kissed her hard enough for it to mean something, fingers trailing lower until they slipped beneath layers of clothing with an ease born from familiarity rather than urgency.

Pauline gasped when Marti's thumb found its target; her hips jerked forward without subtlety as she grabbed onto Marti's shoulder for balance.

"Fuck," Pauline whispered against Marti's mouth before pulling at the buttons of her trousers in search of more contact, more friction, more anything. She didn't have to ask twice. Marti buried herself deeper between tense thighs just as Pauline bit down on a moan hard enough that it escaped past clenched teeth.

It got messy fast: hands grasping at fabric since neither of them cared about wrinkles or consequences; mouths finding skin between hurried movements; muscles tightening beneath Marti's fingers as Pauline rocked forward again and again until tension snapped between them in a shuddering gasp of release muffled by Marti's throat.

Short and sweet.

Marti traced a fingertip along Pauline's lower lip, watching as it parted beneath her touch.

Pauline's lips closed around the offered finger, pulling it into the heat of her mouth, tasting herself without hesitation. Marti kissed her hard, stealing back every last drop, before breaking away and running her tongue across her own bottom lip, considering.

"Marti," Pauline breathed, still catching up to the moment. "You have the magic touch."

Marti smirked. "And you have the magic pussy." One last kiss, short and filthy, before she was washing her hands in the kitchen sink and heading for the living room as if getting wrecked in a back hallway wasn't worth mentioning.

"Where were you?" Evelyn asked as Marti sauntered in.

"Needed the bathroom, then I got lost. You have a very large home, Mrs. Delacroix," Marti said as she looked at a painting she would never comprehend.

"Please, call me Evelyn."

Evelyn and Lori sat across from each other, drinks in hand, conversation low and deliberate. Marti dropped onto the sofa next to Lori, their shoulders knocking together; years of that kind of relationship made physical space irrelevant between them.

Lori's nose twitched as Marti settled in. She turned her head, took a deeper inhale, blinked, and then side-eyed

Marti with a knowing smirk. Yeah. She knew exactly where Marti had been.

Oblivious or just too lost in her own grief to care, Evelyn sighed and swirled her drink in its glass. "Marcus was a philanthropist, you know," she said with practiced wistfulness. "Passionate about local politics; always trying to leave this city better than he found it."

Marti leaned forward before she could stop herself, something between exhaustion and irritation flickering behind her eyes.

Lori nudged her knee against Marti's, amused but silent.

Evelyn kept talking over the ice in her glass clinking against its rim. "He built his empire on fast food: burgers, fries, the American dream with a side of grease," she said with something like pride curling along the edges of regret. "With Ari's help, we expanded into trucking and shipping."

Still swirling that drink between delicate fingers, she stared into it as if waiting for an answer that wasn't coming.

"Pauline, get me my medicine," Evelyn said.

Obediently, Pauline opened a small box and handed Evelyn a small golden inhaler.

Medicine my ass. It was a Shadow inhaler, just fancier.

Like every other junkie, Eleanor took a puff, coughed a little, and handed it back to Pauline.

"It takes the edge off," Evelyn said without guilt.

Marti tilted her head. "Mrs. Delacroix," she said, "did your husband have any enemies?"

A pause stretched out between them: not long enough to be guilt, but just long enough that Marti noticed.

"No," Evelyn said. "Marcus made friends, not enemies." Her lashes fluttered once as she glanced up at them both. "He was well-loved."

Marti hummed low in her throat but didn't bother hiding the skepticism tightening at the corners of her mouth. Marcus Thornfield was neither well-loved nor enemy-free; half this town would've toasted his death if they weren't afraid of being next on someone's list.

"What about vices?" Lori asked, as if she weren't interested but still wanted to check under every rock just in case something crawled out from underneath it. "Drinking? Gambling? Women?"

Evelyn laughed; it didn't reach her eyes. "Nothing like that," she said. "Marcus was a man of integrity."

Marti let silence settle between them for a beat before asking the one question that mattered most right now: "Where were you when he died?"

Evelyn stiffened just enough that only someone staring at her wrists would notice how small tendons pulled tight beneath pearl bracelets when she set down her drink on the table beside them.

She met Marti's gaze head-on but didn't bother keeping the frost out of it this time. "Des Moines," she said. "Visiting family." A single lift of one brow followed: test me. Then: "I have witnesses."

Lori stood a second later, finishing off whatever remained at the bottom of her glass before placing it neatly beside Evelyn with an easy grin that didn't quite reach her eyes either. "We mean nothing by that," she said as she nudged Marti. "But if we didn't ask..."

"Certainly. And since the police asked, no, there was no life insurance."

Marti stood and nodded. "Strange."

Evelyn huffed. "He thought himself invincible."

"We'll see ourselves out," Lori murmured before Evelyn could make some excuse about being tired or having an early morning ahead, before any of them could pretend they weren't all just waiting for someone else to crack first under pressure formalities wouldn't acknowledge outright.

As they stepped toward the hall leading back outside, Evelyn called softly over her shoulder: "Pauline?"

"Yes ma'am, I'll show them out," said the shadow as it melted from one doorway into another, as if she'd been listening all along, or maybe as if she'd known they'd be leaving sooner rather than later.

Pauline didn't hesitate when she pressed herself flush against Marti without pretense or warning; just heat against fabric against muscle memory sharper than any knife-edge suspicion lingering in thick air between them.

"Marcus had someone," Pauline whispered against Marti's jawline, breath warm enough to leave goosebumps trailing up arms already too familiar with bruises pressed into sheets instead of skin.

"He took them out to the pool house," she continued quietly, like confessing sin after hours at an altar meant for anything but salvation.

"Would bring them there regular. But I never saw who." A pause lodged itself thick and unshaken between parted lips before: "I think he was expecting someone that night."

Marti stayed close as exhale met inhale met moment measured in heartbeats against clavicles threatening to betray too much history between two hands still caught somewhere between past lovers and present suspects.

Her mouth hovered near Pauline's pulse point when she let out a husky: "Thank you."

Pauline slid fingers down until they brushed between Marti's legs, not hesitant at all, smiling slow and wicked at how little resistance met fingertips pressing through fabric damp enough to tell its own story.

"No," Pauline whispered back against teeth grazing soft skin this time: "Thank you. But how much will I get?"

Marti grinned sharp as broken glass. The woman was insatiable.

"I'll take an inhaler," she said, completely deflating Marti's ego. Of fucking course she wanted something other than sex. The sex was free. Information never was.

Marti pulled an inhaler out of her pocket and pressed it into Pauline's hand. Pauline smiled until she looked at it.

"This is just a regular one. I want a Golden Shadow inhaler."

Marti quirked an eyebrow. "The fuck is that?"

Pauline sighed, shook her head, and pocketed the inhaler. "It's new. In house. Maybe I'll introduce you."

"I think I want to be golden," Marti said with a laugh.

"Next time," Pauline said with a wink and a tit tweak.

Outside, streetlamps hummed electricity into shadows stretched across pavement still slick from rain hours old but not forgotten yet.

Lori shoved hands deep into coat pockets and fixed Marti with an infuriatingly expectant look before breaking silence stretched too thin between smirks neither had any business wearing so well.

"So," Lori said as they walked toward City Hall to find out exactly how much Thornfield was paying the locals to keep his business to himself.

"Are you gonna give me details or am I just supposed to guess how many times you made poor Pauline pray tonight?"

Marti blew smoke straight past Lori's grin without answering.

Some things were better left unsaid.

But fuck if staying quiet ever stopped Lori from asking anyway.

Chapter 5

The Department of Health reeked of antiseptic and dead ambition; it was the kind of place where even paperwork went to die. Marti slouched in a chair that seemed designed to punish people for existing, her leg bouncing with contained irritation.

Lori sat as if she belonged here. Back straight, hands folded, looking like the responsible secretary while Marti resisted the urge to kneel in front of her and lick her shoes, just to watch the woman squirm.

Marti hated places like this: too clean, too orderly, too full of people who thought "procedure" was holy doctrine instead of an elaborate excuse to do nothing. But Colin Bonner had answers about Marcus Thornfield's perfect fast food joints, and she would endure the bureaucratic hellscape if it meant getting them.

The office door swung open. There he stood: mid-forties, graying at the temples but still clinging to a crisp sports coat as if it gave him authority. He scanned them both with mild curiosity before pasting on a professional smile.

"Marti Starova and Lori Harring?" His voice held that practiced politeness government types used when they wanted you out of their office quickly. "Come on in."

Inside, Bonner's office looked exactly as Marti expected: stale air, walls covered with regulation posters, and a desk drowning in paperwork no one read. Files and manuals stacked high enough to bury whatever conscience he might've once had.

And yet, Marti's gaze flicked across the room. There were cracks in the illusion. Opulence where there shouldn't be any: a gold watch that cost more than her car; an ornate pen that didn't write grocery lists so much as sign off on expensive deals; a framed photo of a yacht so big it might as well have been flipping off every health inspector salary cap in existence.

Government clerks didn't wear tailored suits or collect luxury pens unless they were dipping into something deeper than a paycheck. And Colin Bonner? He was definitely dipping.

Marti dropped into one of the chairs across from him, letting silence stretch between them until discomfort settled in. She wasn't here for small talk.

Bonner cleared his throat: a nervous tic if she ever heard one. He gestured at them both as if they hadn't already made themselves comfortable in his space. "What can I do for you?"

"Marcus Thornfield's dead," Lori said, skipping pleasantries as if they were beneath her notice.

Bonner sighed as if he'd just tasted something sour. "Suicide." He shook his head with the manufactured sadness only men with expensive hobbies could afford. "Tragic."

Marti wasn't buying it, but she didn't call him on it either. She leaned forward, matching his expression with one friendlier as she lied through her teeth:

"His business partner sent me over for health records on Thornfield's restaurants," she said. "Seems Marcus didn't keep any files at the office."

Colin hesitated too long before reaching for his drawers. "Let me check my records."

Marti nodded and leaned back, studying him while he fumbled through paperwork he probably knew wasn't there. Her eyes dragged from his wrist (the glittering watch) to his desk (the pen fit for signing someone else's future away) to the yacht picture screaming Look how rich I am.

Yeah, Colin Bonner was living above his means. The real question was why.

Beside her, Lori sat still except for her fingers tapping against one knee: an unspoken conversation waiting to happen between them. Marti caught the movement and gave Lori a slight nod: Let's see how deep this guy's bullshit goes.

"Nice pen," Lori said, eyes flicking to the sleek Montblanc on Colin Bonner's desk. "And that watch. Fancy."

Colin's jaw twitched. His fingers curled over his wrist as if she might snatch the damn thing off him. Then he didn't bother lying.

"Thornfield paid me," he said, voice steady but laced with something between pride and desperation. "Made sure his restaurants passed inspection without trouble. He was generous. The extra cash helped."

Marti arched a brow. "So you were on Thornfield's payroll." She leaned forward, letting the silence stretch until he started to sweat before adding, "Did you kill him?"

Colin recoiled. "What? No! Why would I? Thornfield's death puts me in a bad spot; I might not get those payments anymore. If his companies tank, that money's gone."

Marti exchanged a glance with Lori, who looked unimpressed. "You're not worried about losing your job for taking bribes?"

He laughed. "Lady, I'd probably get fired if I didn't take them. Everyone: politicians, inspectors, managers. Everyone gets their cut. Refuse, and people start wondering if you're a rat."

Marti snorted. "Real inspiring workplace culture."

"Yeah, well," Colin shrugged. "You wanted honesty."

"Anybody have a real reason to want Thornfield dead?"

Colin sat back and folded his arms over his chest, looking comfortable considering the situation. "Hundreds," he said. "He was an asshole." Then, as if remembering how normal conversation worked: "Coffee?"

Marti stood up before Lori could answer. "Nah. Thanks for your time."

"You don't want the paperwork?"

"Please forward it to Ari Stirling," Marti laughed as she picked that asshole getting an unexpected delivery of restaurant status reports.

Lori followed her out of Colin Bonner's cramped little kingdom of corruption and into the wide halls of City Hall: cold marble underfoot, walls gleaming with bureaucratic indifference. The place reeked of stale coffee and politics gone bad.

Halfway down the staircase, Lori froze. Marti nearly barreled into her.

"There he is," Lori hissed.

Marti followed her gaze straight to Mayor Bruce Garrison, oozing sleaze in an expensive suit and sporting an unnatural tan that looked like Cheeto dust under the fluorescent lights.

Lori crossed her arms. "Think he's anti-gay for votes or for fun?"

Marti tilted her head, studying the man who wanted to scrub queerness off city property as if it was graffiti instead of people's lives.

"Oh, totally for shits and giggles," she said.

Garrison turned. Lori transformed from spectator to main event.

"Hey Garrison!" she called out. "I know your secrets!"

The mayor paused mid-stride, coated in the kind of fake charm that got men like him elected despite everyone knowing better.

Marti leaned in toward Lori. "Do we actually know his secrets?"

Lori's grin was all teeth. "No," she whispered back. "But it sounds good."

Garrison recovered; polished politician mode activated as he sauntered toward them as if they were adoring fans instead of two angry women.

"Ladies," he drawled, offering a hand neither of them had any intention of taking. "What an unexpected pleasure."

Marti took in his unshakable confidence and felt an itch in her fists.

This conversation was going to be fun.

"Let me guess," Garrison said, each syllable dripping condescension. "You're a couple of angry lesbians mad about the Pride flag ban. Did I nail it?"

"Go fuck yourself," Lori shot back, and Marti, despite everything, let out a short laugh. Garrison's smug grin widened as if he thought he was winning. Cute.

Then he pulled out his phone and started recording himself.

Marti and Lori exchanged a look. Oh, this was going to be good.

"Ladies," Garrison intoned, voice rich with artificial gravitas. "Falls City stands at a crossroads. Our once-thriving community is under siege: criminals roam unchecked, the moral fabric of our society frays, and decent hardworking citizens are left defenseless."

Marti resisted rolling her eyes. Classic fear-mongering bullshit. She knew where this was going.

"A city under siege," Garrison went on, almost reverent now, as if he was delivering a sermon instead of spewing whatever slop his speechwriter cooked up for him this morning. "And who leads this charge? Who demands more than their fair share while contributing nothing? The gays."

Marti snorted. "The gays? Oh. My. God. The gays!"

A few people had gathered now, office drones smelling an excuse to postpone actual work for another ten minutes. Not a riotous mob, but they were listening. And that was enough to be dangerous.

Garrison took their silence as encouragement and forged ahead, stepping closer, angling the camera for maximum dramatic effect. "Patriots of Falls City," he declared, "we will not be intimidated by minority interests pushing radical agendas."

Lori muttered something under her breath that sounded like dick cheese, but Marti wasn't sure and didn't ask because.

"The death of Marcus Thornfield," Garrison proclaimed with his theatrical pause, "was only the beginning."

What the fuck?

Lori stiffened beside her. "Did he just say Thornfield?" she whispered, voice sharp with something close to actual concern.

Marti didn't answer. She locked eyes on Garrison, watching him pace, turning his words into something bigger than himself, as if they could slip into people's ears and take root like an infection.

"You've all heard the stories," Garrison continued, like this was some damn fireside chat instead of public character assassination in real time. "Marcus Thornfield may have appeared a normal, even kind man; a philanthropist with deep pockets and a bleeding heart. But behind closed doors? A different man entirely."

The crowd murmured: a ripple of uncertainty passing through them as they digested what their mayor was spoon-feeding them with such polish.

Marti tightened her grip on her cigarette and thought. If Garrison was saying this now, if he was comfortable enough to spin Thornfield's death into some bullshit morality tale, what did that mean?

"Thornfield's so-called philanthropy?" Garrison pressed. "A smokescreen for corruption at its worst! He used his wealth not for charity but control! Manipulation! For the gays!" He let those words settle before going in for the kill: "And let's be honest, it was only a matter of time before it caught up with him."

The audience murmurs grew louder. Some nodded along as if this whole thing made perfect sense because of course it did when you framed it right.

Justice had been served. That's what he wanted them to believe.

Marti lit a cigarette and pulled out her phone as Lori leaned close enough that her breath tickled Marti's ear.

"He knows something." Lori's voice was tight with fury.

Marti tapped fast, commentary flowing.

Bruce Garrison had just admitted on record: Marcus Thornfield hadn't died in some random accident.

He'd been murdered.

And Bruce fucking Garrison said he knew why.

There was no way he was telling the truth, but the question was, what was he trying to hide?

The rain hit the windshield in fat drops, smeared by the wipers into greasy streaks. Marti's fingers drummed against the steering wheel, cigarette dangling from her lips as she and Lori sat parked outside City Hall. The city stretched around them, neon glistening on wet pavement, too quiet for how loud her thoughts were.

"You catch how confident he sounded?" Lori asked, kicking her boots up on the dashboard without asking. "Like he knew something we don't."

Marti took a drag, let the nicotine sit in her lungs before exhaling. "Yeah. Smug little shit acted like Thornfield's death was murder and it's common knowledge."

Lori let out a low breath, staring out into the rain. "So why not pressure the cops to investigate? He said Thornfield supported some kind of gay cabal, think that was it?"

"Or," Marti said, flicking ash onto the floor, "he's in on it."

Silence stretched between them. Then Lori gave a short laugh. "That's one hell of a leap."

Marti tilted her head. "Is it? Thornfield's death was staged to look like a suicide, but without the gun. What if Garrison wasn't just yapping? What if he knows he is untouchable?"

Lori sucked in a breath through her teeth. "Shit."

Exactly.

Raindrops ran crooked paths down the windshield as silence settled again, heavy with uneasy possibilities.

Marti rolled down her window and flicked out the rest of her cigarette before rubbing at her eyes. Too many loose threads, too many angles that didn't line up. But that could wait till tomorrow.

"I'm taking you home," Marti said as she started the car.

Lori hummed, settling back into the passenger seat with a stretch that did nothing to hide the way her dress rode up her thigh. "You make it sound like a punishment."

Marti glanced over, half-amused. "Depends. You planning to behave?"

Lori tilted her head, lips curving. "What's your preference?"

Marti chuckled, drumming her fingers against the wheel as they idled at a red light. She flicked a glance at Lori's bare legs, the smooth line of her knee bent just enough to make the hem of that damn dress a whole situation. "You do that on purpose?"

Lori smirked. "Do what?"

Marti sighed, shaking her head as the light turned green. "You know what."

"You know," she said, voice teasing, "if you're so distracted, I could always drive."

Marti snorted. "No chance in hell."

Lori grinned. "What, afraid I'll crash your precious heap of junk?"

Marti shot her a sidelong look. "No, afraid you'll start adjusting the mirrors to check yourself out and we'll end up wrapped around a light pole."

Lori laughed. "At least I'd die looking good."

Marti just shook her head.

They pulled up in front of Lori's building, the city pressing in around them: streetlights buzzing, late-night pedestrians lingering, the faint scent of rain on warm pavement.

"Well," Marti said, turning to Lori with a smirk that felt more natural than thinking about a murder they couldn't pin down yet, "another night in this goddamn city. You home alone?"

Lori snorted, stretching before reaching for the door handle. "Unless you're planning on staying."

Marti huffed out a laugh but shook her head. "Tempting offer, Lori, but I've got work to do that doesn't include my secretary."

Lori raised an eyebrow as she stepped out of the car, rain catching in the dark strands of her hair. "Right," she drawled. "Because nothing says 'productive night' like drowning yourself in Shadow."

Marti rolled her eyes but didn't deny it.

Lori leaned back down into the open window. "Try to stay clean tonight."

"I'll try." It wasn't a promise.

Lori sighed but didn't push it further. Just tapped twice on the roof of the car and walked toward her building.

Marti watched until Lori's ass disappeared through the front doors before she put the car in gear and pulled back onto the road.

Falls City swallowed her whole again: neon halos bouncing off puddles, alleyways curling like dark veins through its heart. Somewhere beneath all that light and shadow was an answer waiting to be found.

She just had to make it through tonight first.

And right now?

Her craving for Shadow clawed at her ribs worse than any mystery could.

Chapter 6

Marti sucked in a breath, let it out slow. The taste of Shadow still lingered at the back of her throat, a ghost of desire slipping through her fingers. She wasn't going to use tonight. Probably.

The sex with Pauline had been fine: good, even. No amount of sweat and skin could quiet the thing inside her, gnawing at her insides like an animal left too long in a cage.

"Fuck." She dragged a hand down her face, exhaling smoke she hadn't inhaled. Shadow was worse than any lover she'd ever had. Always the same deal: temporary relief, long-term destruction.

A gust of wind carried the scent of cinnamon and butter through the streets, cutting through city grime and exhaust fumes as if a knife slipping between ribs. Marti knew that smell.

Lia. She hadn't realized she driven herself to Fischer's bakery.

She glanced across the street. The bakery glowed like some goddamn beacon in the dark, a mirage in a city built on concrete and bad decisions. Her pulse kicked up, though whether from want or warning, she wasn't sure.

What once belonged to Billie River now belonged to Lia Fischer: the bakery and Marti.

Lia's place was warm light and sugar-dusted promises; everything Marti wasn't. She never had been. But it was what she needed right now: something sweet to chase down all the bitterness twisting inside her chest.

She was getting nowhere on the investigation on Thornfield. And on Henry Gardner. She hoped she could get somewhere with Lia.

She flicked her cigarette into the gutter and crossed the street before she could talk herself out of it.

The brass handle was cold under her palm as she pushed inside, the doorbell chiming overhead like some polite announcement of her intrusion. The air hit her: spiced apples, fresh bread, heat curling around her skin in soft contrast to the chill outside.

Somewhere behind the counter, Lia's voice slid over her like silk stretched too tight over steel. "Well, well." A smirk bled into every syllable. "Look what the cat dragged in."

Marti's lips twitched before she could stop them, a reflex buried deep in old habits and past sins. "Just passing through."

"Yeah?" Lia raised a brow, hands moving without thought as she stacked pastries onto a tray. "Didn't think sugar was your vice."

Marti's gaze dragged over Lia's hands, long fingers dusted with flour, practiced movements honed from shaping dough into something worth wanting. Her pulse did that thing again. "Only yours."

Lia hummed low in her throat as if she knew exactly what Marti meant but wasn't about to give anything away for free. She slid an apple turnover onto a plate and nudged it toward her across the counter. "Looks like you could use something nice for once."

Marti hesitated because this wasn't nice, not really. She picked up the pastry anyway, tearing off a piece just to have something other than Lia's eyes to focus on. Warm butter and spiced fruit hit her tongue, rich enough to make her forget, for half a second, how fucked everything else was outside these walls.

Lia leaned one hip against the counter, watching her with sharp amusement wrapped in soft edges. "You look like hell," she said, but there was weight beneath it that didn't quite match her smirk. "Shadow?"

Marti swallowed hard enough to feel it burn all the way down and licked crumbs off her thumb before answering. "Something like that."

Lia didn't push; not yet. Something passed between them anyway: something old and worn at the edges but still fucking dangerous if either of them got too close again.

And Marti? She'd always been shit at keeping distance where Lia Fisher was concerned.

"Sweetness doesn't last in this city," Marti said, eyes locked on Lia's as she took a bite. The pastry flaked apart between her teeth, buttery and warm, but the apple hit sharp, tart enough to make her jaw tighten. A shock of something half-forgotten flickered through her, as if memory itself stirred awake.

Lia watched her, dark eyes not missing a thing. "Maybe," she allowed, tilting her head, "but not every-thing gets swallowed by the night. Sometimes, all it takes is a little light."

Marti snorted, wiping crumbs from her fingers against her jeans. "Yeah? Good luck finding any." She let her gaze drag over Lia's face, searching for something: deception, pity. All she found was that quiet fucking sincerity that had always made her weak in the knees. She didn't have time for that.

"It lasts longer than you think." Lia's voice dipped low as she leaned over the counter, conspiratorial and inviting. "And sometimes the best light comes from the most unexpected places."

Marti arched a brow. "What is this? You volunteering to be my personal lighthouse?"

Lia smiled slow. "Only if you'll have just one."

Something tight coiled at the base of Marti's spine: familiar and unhelpful. She'd been burned before by Lia. More than once. But Lia had always been fire and warmth together, and Marti had never been smart about keeping herself from reaching toward the heat.

"Maybe," she muttered, clearing her throat as if that would make it sound less pathetic. "Just maybe."

The corner of Lia's mouth twitched as if she knew exactly how much of a fucking mess Marti was inside but wasn't about to press it. Instead, she reached across the counter, palm brushing over the back of Marti's hand with enough pressure to linger. The warmth sank deep, spreading through Marti's veins like something dangerous.

She needed out of this moment before it pulled her under. She needed focus. She needed something real to hold onto besides old ghosts and bad decisions dressed as second chances.

"Tell me about Marcus Thornfield," she said around another mouthful of pastry, swallowing down more than sugar and spice with the words. Her tone cut through whatever had been building between them. "You must've known him."

Lia's expression shuttered; not completely, not yet. There was something guarded in the way her shoulders tensed that told Marti she'd hit something raw beneath all that charm.

Once upon a time, Lia had run one of Falls City's more infamous brothels: the kind built on secrets as much as sex. That was how they'd met; business first, then something else until it all fell apart like everything else in Marti's life eventually did.

Lia exhaled and leaned closer, enough for the warmth between them to turn razor-edged again. "You're such a bastard sometimes, you know that?" Her voice was soft but laced with something sharp beneath it, something almost like hurt if Marti let herself believe it for even a second. "I thought you were here for me."

"You've called me worse," Marti said because deflecting was easier than dealing with whatever stared back at her from behind Lia's narrowed gaze. She licked apple from her lip and shrugged one shoulder like none of this mattered anyway. It was probably a lie even as she said it: "I'm working his death."

"I heard it was suicide," Lia said, as if testing how much of this conversation mattered to Marti outside of whatever history they were both pretending didn't exist between them anymore.

Marti popped the rest of the turnover into her mouth and chewed before replying. "I was hired to make sure."

For a moment, nothing but silence stretched between them, thick as Shadow-smoke curling against streetlights outside bakery windows. Lia sighed through gritted teeth and shook her head as if she should've known better than to think Marti showing up at her counter meant anything but business.

"Thornfield had secrets," she admitted, voice low enough to feel intimate despite itself. "More than just this place." Her lips quirked into something wry as she added: "And trust me when I say he had his fingers in more pies than just this one."

Marti tilted her head, chewing on Lia's words the same way she chewed through the last of the turnover. "You talking about the bakery or your body?"

Lia's mouth pulled into something dangerous and amused. "It wasn't mine he was interested in."

Marti whistled, unable to process how anyone couldn't want to fuck that body.

Marti snorted, licking sugar from her thumb. "Guessing Thornfield wasn't just buying croissants."

"His dealings were expansive," Lia said, fingers tracing shapes on the counter. "Arms trade, trafficking, money laundering; if there was a black market, he had a hand in it."

Marti sighed. "Yeah, yeah, he was a piece of shit. Who wanted him dead?"

Lia's eyes flicked downward. Something softer crept onto her face before she shoved it back down where it belonged. "Plenty of people. But if you want motive? Best place to start is with the ones closest to him."

"Wife. Business partners." Marti took another sip of coffee, letting Lia's words settle like grounds at the bottom of a cup. But something about the way she said it, too smooth, too rehearsed, made alarms go off in Marti's skull.

Lia exhaled, all patience and secrets. "Perhaps." A smile followed. Slow, knowing, curling up like cigarette smoke.

"Or maybe there were people who knew him far better than they'd ever admit."

Marti leaned forward, letting the scent of burned espresso and something floral mix between them. "Say what you mean."

Lia didn't answer right away. Instead, she reached for an oversized mug and filled it to the brim with steaming black coffee before sliding it across the counter to Marti's waiting hands. "Thornfield had preferences," she said. "And some powerful people might've felt exposed if those preferences became public knowledge."

Marti set down her cup with too much force. "Blackmail," she muttered; the word settled between them like an inconvenient truth. She ran her tongue along her teeth before finishing her thought: "You think someone killed him to keep their secrets buried?"

Lia lifted one shoulder in an elegant shrug, but her eyes stayed sharp beneath lowered lashes. "It's possible." She paused. "But I also think Thornfield had a gift for making enemies. And there was no shortage of people who wanted him out of the picture."

Marti tapped her fingers against her mug twice before cutting straight to it: "Like who?"

Lia hesitated just long enough for Marti to catch it, one heartbeat too long before answering, not enough to be obvious unless you were looking for it. Then:

"He was a regular at my old place," Lia murmured, gaze shifting toward the window as if staring past the rain-streaked glass would somehow distance her from whatever came next. "But he wasn't just there for the women."

Marti raised an eyebrow. The bakery smelled like caramelized sugar and fresh bread and whatever this conversation was turning into: something darker beneath all that sweetness.

"Adults?"

Lia scoffed and rolled her eyes upward as if she couldn't believe she had to clarify this part for Marti. "Don't be a dick," she said before lowering her voice: "I only worked with adults." She paused. "He liked twinks." Another pause. "All legal, but young looking men."

"Skinny ones," Marti guessed, piecing it together from years of reading between lines people didn't want spoken aloud.

Something flickered through Lia's expression: a quiet confirmation that didn't need words to land its weight in Marti's gut.

Marti exhaled, gears in her brain grinding against each other as they worked through this new shape Thornfield was taking in front of her. Garrison hinted that Thornfield supported the queer community, but it went beyond that. Desires locked behind expensive doors and shuttered windows; hands in everything but not enough places to keep himself alive.

"Anyone else know about this?" She kept her voice level though she knew secrets this volatile never stayed secret forever.

"A handful," Lia admitted after a hesitation, a small one but still there, before adding: "But Thornfield never took chances with his reputation."

That made Marti laugh; dry and humorless because nothing about this was funny. "Yeah? How'd he pull that off?"

"He wore masks," Lia said simply, her voice so casual about it that it almost slipped past unnoticed in all its implications until she followed it up: "And when it comes to flesh and power? Even oaths cracked open eventually."

"Masks? As in, masks?" Marti said as she waved a hand in front of her face.

Lia nodded.

Marti turned that over in her mind like a puzzle piece someone jammed into the wrong spot just hard enough to make it fit, for now, before finally saying what need-ed saying: "Well fuck. But sucking dick doesn't get you killed. Not in Falls City." Marti flicked her cigarette ash into the half-empty coffee cup she'd forgotten about hours ago. "He had money. A mask. How's that a problem for anyone?"

"Depends," Lia said, voice low, unreadable. "Thornfield didn't just indulge; he collected. And not just for fun."

Marti exhaled and leaned back in her chair. "Ah, fuck. He was blackmailing people, wasn't he?"

Lia gave a slow nod. "He built himself a vault of secrets, each one more damning than the last. Powerful men will-ing to pay for silence. People too scared to fight back."

"And if they did?"

"They lost," Lia said.

Marti dragged a hand through her hair and laughed, sharp and mirthless. "Who else knew?"

"Hard to say," Lia admitted after a pause. "His inner circle, if you could call it that." She didn't meet Marti's eyes when she added, "People he trusted. People he owned."

Marti's gaze sharpened. "You helped him." It wasn't a question. She was getting fed up with the bullshit.

Lia looked up, dark eyes steady. "I ran a business."

"That's not an answer," Marti said.

Lia tilted her head, considering her next words as if they mattered beyond whatever fragile thread still tethered them together. "I'm not a rat," she said, quiet but sure.

Marti scoffed and stood up so fast her chair scraped against the floor. "Yeah? Not your business?"

Lia turned away, watching the rain snake down the bakery window as if it had somewhere better to be. "Mine has always been survival Marti, you know that."

"No shit," Marti muttered, digging into her pocket until her fingers brushed metal: cold and familiar and just as much of a problem as everything else in this goddamn city. Shadow called to her like it always did. Just one hit would clear her head, make all of this easier. But another problem was standing right in front of her in worn denim and cheap perfume and eyes that saw too fucking much.

Lia sighed without looking at her. She knew Marti far too well. "Your devil comes between us."

Marti clenched her fist around the inhaler before forcing herself to let go, forcing herself to focus on something else: how close Lia was now, how easy it would be to close the distance if she wanted to make another bad decision tonight.

She wanted Lia's face, hands, mouth; the taste of smoke and something sharp beneath it that might've been regret if either of them had time for such things anymore.

The rain outside softened into a whisper against glass. Inside, everything was too loud: her pulse hammering against her ribs, Lia's breath catching in something that might've been anticipation or warning or both. Marti took one step forward without thinking. Then another. Fuck thinking when it only made things worse.

"Damn," Marti said without meaning to say anything at all. Then softer, rougher: "I want to kiss you."

Lia didn't move, didn't blink, just watched her with something unreadable flickering behind those eyes before finally breathing out:

"No." She moved back.

"There's always been something between us," Lia said, voice rough, as if the words hurt coming out. "Something bigger than all the bullshit: the lies, the secrets." Her fingers flexed at her sides, wanting, needing. "You said you'd quit. Get clean. But I know you're still using." She let out a sharp breath. "I fucking hate you for it." A beat. "And I want you anyway." Her gaze flicked to Marti's pocket. "You have it, don't you? An inhaler?"

Marti didn't answer. Just stared, pulse thrumming in her throat, the weight of everything between them pressing down like the rain outside: steady, relentless. One step forward and she could forget. Just for a second. Sink into

Lia's heat and let it drown out the rest: Shadow, regret, every rotten thing she'd done to get here.

But Lia had already left once. And Marti wasn't stupid enough to pretend that didn't mean anything.

"Yeah." Her voice barely made it past her lips. "I have a few." She swallowed hard. "I don't think I can stop."

Silence stretched between them. Then Lia moved, slow and sure, closing the space until Marti could count every dark lash framing those unreadable eyes.

Lia's hand moved fast: sharp, stinging, a slap that snapped Marti's head to the side. "Jesus," Marti muttered, more startled than hurt, her pulse kicking up. But before she could say anything else, Lia caught her chin, forced her to face her again; eyes dark, lips parted, breath unsteady.

"Then kiss me," she said.

The kiss hit hard: desperate, all teeth and tongue and too many things they would never say out loud. Marti fisted her hands into the fabric at Lia's hips, held tight as if she could keep her there if she just tried hard enough.

For a second, nothing else existed: not the storm outside or Shadow curling its claws around Marti's ribs, not even the mess they were both tangled in.

Just this.

Then it ended: too fast, too much. They pulled apart just enough for air, heads bowed together as if neither of them knew what came next.

Lia spoke first. "Whatever happens now, you're on your own." Her breath still tasted like coffee and regret and something softer underneath that Marti couldn't name. "I can't do this if Shadow is in the way."

Marti closed her eyes. Nodded once.

Clean and sober.

It wasn't a promise so much as an echo of what Lia wanted to hear.

She stepped back before she did something even stupider than kissing her again. "Thanks for the food." The words barely landed before she turned and walked away.

Chapter 7

Dawn clawed its way through thin curtains, smearing weak light over Marti's wreck of a room. She groaned and rolled onto her side, Shadow's phantom warmth still coiled around her like a bad habit. Cold air bit at her skin. Reality, the bastard, was back.

She swung her legs over the bed, feet slamming into wood that had no right being so cold. The clock on the nightstand blinked 9:23 PM.

Had she done anything useful during daylight? Marti couldn't remember.

Too late for remembering. Too late to undo last night. The streets below were ready and waiting: vendors hawking shit resembling food, rustling newspapers, the city grinding forward with or without her.

Marti rubbed the heel of her hand against one eye. "Fuck." She didn't have time for this. She didn't have time for anything these days, not with Thornfield's name stinking up her life like something rotting under the floorboards. She stripped and put on new clothes, or at least clothes that didn't stand up on their own. She settled the holster against her hip from habit more than need. It used to be a comfort: the weight, the steel. Now it was just another thing she couldn't let go of.

Lia would be pissed if she knew about last night.

Or maybe just disappointed. That was worse.

"Maybe tonight," Marti said to no one, her voice flat enough to make it true. "Maybe I'll stop tonight."

The mirror laughed in her face. She was too sharp around the edges, too tired in the eyes, as if she were looking at a stranger who knew all her worst secrets and wasn't impressed by any of them. Her reflection tilted its head just like Lia did when she caught Marti in a lie.

Marti sneered at herself and turned away before it could get worse.

Marti got into her car, hit dial, and drove. Rat was unreliable, uninformed and useless; often how Marti felt.

"Rat?"

The voice on the other end was tired, the sound of old files rustling through a low-quality connection. "Yeah?" came the voice. "Who's asking?"

"Marti Starova. I need a favor. You know the name Henry Gardner? He's missing. I'm trying to find his last known whereabouts."

A beat of silence followed. Then the voice grew cautious. "I don't know if I can help with that. He owes money. Big time."

"Rat, my man, we both know if anything, you owe him." Marti's grip on the steering wheel tightened. "I'm not asking about debts. I'm asking where he is."

She could hear the man shift on the other end. He wasn't ready to spill everything, but Marti was used to people who wanted to talk once they realized how serious she was.

"I'll make it worth your time," she added. "Information for information."

"Shadow."

"Fuck off!" Marti shouted at a pedestrian who crossed with the green light as she drove through the red.

"Fuck you, too!"

"No Rat, not you. Some other asshole. You want the Shadow?" Marti said. She felt sorry for the guy. But he was an asshole.

"Yeah. Okay. We can meet. I got something for you on him."

He wanted to meet at Gung Ho. That meant he was either feeling lucky or suicidal; Gardner owned that place, and neither of them belonged anywhere near it.

Falls City's wind sliced through its streets like it had a personal grudge against everyone still standing upright after midnight. The pavement shimmered under sickly yellow streetlights; grime layered thick enough that even the shadows looked dirty. Marti pulled her jacket tighter around herself and kept walking because stopping wasn't an option anymore: not when Shadow still whispered promises in the back of her skull, not when Henry was missing, not when Thornfield's killer was still breathing free air, not when she needed the money so bad.

Gung Ho smelled like sweat and desperation mixed with second-hand regrets: the kind of place where bad decisions came cheap and nobody asked twice if you wanted to be left alone. The door thudded shut behind her, sealing off the cold but offering nothing close to warmth in return.

She lit up before scanning the room; no one gave a shit about laws here, least of all Marti. She needed to figure out who was carrying a weapon. She figured that was everyone. Her gun wouldn't stand out. Smoke curled between her fingers as she exhaled, another bad habit she wasn't ready to quit, and let her gaze sweep across hunched backs and tired eyes pretending not to notice her arrival.

There he was in the corner booth, nursing something amber and strong enough to burn going down. Marty slid onto the cracked vinyl seat across from him without waiting for an invitation, cigarette dangling between two fingers as she raised an eyebrow in greeting.

"Talk fast," she said, her voice like old whiskey and twice as rough. "I'm short on patience."

Rat smirked, showing yellowed teeth and bad memory. "Marti Starova, darkening my doorstep yet again." His voice rasped like sandpaper on bone, scraping at her nerves. Beady eyes flicked over her face, cataloging the shadows under her eyes, the sharp angles of her cheekbones. "Looks like life's been kicking you around."

Marti took a drag from her cigarette and leveled him with a stare cold enough to freeze hell. "Cut the crap, Rat. You got something for me or not?"

He chuckled. "Name like Gardner carries weight; lotta whispers, lotta ghosts." He swirled his drink, the ice clinking against glass. "Rumor says his dad's got enemies in high places: the kind that don't forgive."

"Spare me the bedtime stories," she said. "Give me something real before I decide you're wasting my time."

Rat spread his hands in mock innocence. "Damn, Starova. You used to be more fun before you lost your badge." He leaned in, his voice dropping as if sharing a secret. "There's a baccarat game running out of the Gung Ho. Not your average round of cards: this one's invitation-only, hundred crisp minimum buy-in. Word is, Henry lost big."

Marti snorted. "Here? In this shithole?" She glanced around at the bar's peeling wallpaper and warped wooden beams sagging under years of cigarette smoke and broken promises. The walls were dressed in faded posters no one had cared to replace, their edges curling inward as if trying to fold in on themselves and disappear. A ceiling fan turned overhead like a man dragging himself out of bed after a three-day bender. It moved, but barely.

She exhaled through her nose. "I don't buy it."

Rat shrugged. "Doesn't matter if you do or don't. What matters is what happens when someone loses more than they can afford." He tilted his head toward a door near the back of the room, its paint chipped away by time and neglect. "That's where they play."

Marti crushed out her cigarette on the table and pushed herself to her feet without another word. If Rat was lying, or worse, feeding her breadcrumbs just to watch her chase ghosts, she'd make sure he regretted it. She crossed the room and gripped the doorknob tight as she shoved it open.

The sharp bite of cleaning solution hit first: bleach and something citrusy fighting for dominance over stale beer and old smoke. Fluorescents flickered overhead as she slapped at the light switch, illuminating a supply closet stuffed with mops, plastic bottles cluttering the floor like discarded hopes and cheap afterthoughts.

A bucket half-full of murky water sat stagnant in a sink so rusted it looked diseased. No poker table, no velvet-lined chairs filled with desperate men throwing around money as if they could buy back their dignity.

Just dust and disappointment. Staring her down like an old enemy come home to roost.

She turned and stalked back toward Rat's booth, rage simmering beneath her skin. He was fidgeting before she sat back down, fingers drumming an uneven rhythm on the tabletop, eyes darting between her face and the exit.

"What the fuck was that?" she asked, flicking ash off her sleeve as smoke curled between them like a warning shot. She'd been hoping for an opening: something solid she could sink into and bury herself inside until she clawed out an answer worth having. This was just another dead end dressed up pretty with false promises and wasted time.

Rat's smile was too quick, too forced, stretched thin across his face like plastic wrap. He licked his chapped lips, a nervous tic she'd seen a hundred times before when he was coming down and desperate for his next fix.

"What's wrong? No game?" His voice cracked, betraying the confident facade.

Marti pulled her gun and pressed it against Rat's forehead. Color drained from his face.

"Shit, alright," he stammered, hands shooting up, trembling. "I was just telling you what I heard. Didn't wanna check myself, on account of not wanting my brains on the pavement." His pupils were pinpricks despite the dim lighting, sweat beading along his hairline.

Marti shoved away from the booth; chair legs scraped loud enough to make him flinch. "You're a waste of my fucking time."

"Yeah? But you still," he swallowed hard, voice desperate now, "you still gotta pay me for it. We had a deal." His eyes flicked to her pocket where she kept her inhalers, not trying to hide his need anymore.

She knew. She'd been played. Rat hadn't given her shit worth knowing; he was so desperate for Shadow that he'd sell her rain in a storm if it meant getting another hit.

"Rat, you didn't tell me anything real."

"I know, I know," he said, rubbing his face as if he could scrub some shame out of himself. It didn't work. "But can't you see? I'm drowning out here, Marti. That inhaler is my lighthouse. Just one. Just one more to keep the dark off me." His voice cracked on the last word. "Please."

Marti stared at him, at the hollowed-out thing he'd become, until something twisted in her gut. Not pity, because she wasn't that kind of person; not anger either, because that would mean she expected better from him. Just exhaustion. He turned that look back on her and saw something in it he didn't like.

"Don't look at me like that," he snapped. "The only difference between you and me is that secretary of yours pulling your ass out of the gutter." He leaned close enough to stink up her air with desperation. "I've seen her saving you before, Marti. You and me? We ain't different."

A slow chill crawled up her spine. Bastard wasn't wrong, not entirely. She was getting worse; Shadow sank its claws deep while she pretended she wasn't bleeding out from it. And now, with Lia gone, Lori might be all she had left keeping her upright instead of face-down in some alley.

Wordless, Marti reached into her pocket and flipped an inhaler onto the table. Rat snatched it midair like a starving dog catching scraps.

"Appreciate it," he muttered before scrambling out the door to chase his next oblivion.

Marti exhaled smoke through clenched teeth and followed him out into the night. The wind hit hard as she stepped onto the street, slapping her hair into her eyes as if nature wanted to smack her upside the head tonight. She ignored it and kept walking, pulling thoughts apart as fast as they formed. Why send her sniffing after this lead if there was nothing there? Was Rat wrong about the bar but right about the room? Somewhere out there was a bastard she had to find, but Marti wasn't about to start guessing where to dig next just because Rat had fed her bullshit for a fix.

Her boots echoed against wet pavement as Falls City swallowed her whole again: a ghost moving through shadows in search of something solid to grab onto before she disappeared.

The car was warm and dry. It was time to switch cases. It wouldn't take long to see the widow again. She tongued the inside of her cheek and muttered: "Thornfield, it's your turn."

The headlights snapped off in front of the Delacroix home and she trudged up the front stairs.

She hesitated before shaking loose from whatever instincts screamed at her not to go knocking on that particular door tonight, not because Delacroix was dangerous, but because Evelyn might be home; and if Evelyn was home, Pauline might be too.

And if Pauline was there? Information wasn't the only thing Marti stood to get tonight.

Marti squared her shoulders and knocked. The sound ricocheted through the quiet night, too loud, too final. No turning back now.

The door cracked open enough for Evelyn Delacroix's glare to knife through the gap. Since she was answering herself, Pauline was gone. That made things easier. Or worse.

"Starova," Evelyn said, voice clipped, precise: weaponized disdain wrapped in silk. "What the hell do you want?"

Marti smiled like she had all the time in the world and none of the bruises from earlier. "Life's full of surprises, Mrs. Delacroix," she said, dry as gin and twice as bitter. "May I come in?"

"No." Evelyn's lip curled. "You're a fucking animal. I saw what you did. I have cameras everywhere." Her voice sharpened with each accusation as if she could peel Marti apart with just her tongue. "I had to get my goddamned kitchen professionally cleaned because of you! She's not here."

Well, that explained the hostility. Marti shoved aside the flicker of something close to guilt and pressed on. "I'm here to ask your permission to speak to your company's staff tomorrow," she said, watching for any sign of a crack in Evelyn's armor. "They might know something: someone who was harassing your husband." A pause for effect. "I'd like your permission."

It shifted something in Evelyn, just enough for Marti to see her ego stretch its limbs and preen at the attention. A calculated risk, but it landed where it needed to.

"Fine," Evelyn said after a long beat, chin lifting as if she'd decided to grant Marti some grand favor instead of just doing what they both knew she was always going to do anyway. "You can speak to my staff."

Marti tilted her head forward in something resembling gratitude. "May I come in?"

Evelyn let out a sharp bark of laughter and slammed the door instead.

"Thought not," Marti muttered as she turned away. She caught a scent: something foul, dead. Fuck. Sniffing at her coat made her wince. She reeked; smoke, sweat, stale beer, maybe whatever the hell she'd sat in at the Gung Ho earlier. Perfect.

Yeah, that's why Evelyn didn't want her in the house.

At least there was one advantage to being turned away like a stray dog. Evelyn thought she would leave; foolish woman. So Marti headed to the pool house out back. Pauline had said Thornfield indulged someone back there. Maybe there was something.

She headed into the yard, tracking past the glowing perimeter lights of the pool when a noise snapped behind her: too light for danger but too deliberate to ignore.

Marti pivoted, fists tightening out of habit.

Pauline stood there, arms crossed, looking her up and down with that infuriating smile curving at the edges of her mouth.

"What are you doing?" Pauline asked but kept her voice low.

"Following up," Marti said, though she wasn't sure whose anymore. "You said Thornfield would see someone in the pool house." She took a step closer because she could, grinning when Pauline didn't move away. "Evelyn wouldn't let me in, so I thought I'd sniff around."

Pauline tsked and tipped her head as if she was considering something dangerous or delicious: or both.

"Sniff around? Like a damned dog?" Pauline murmured.

Marti smirked at that because yeah, maybe she was.

Pauline sighed before stepping close enough that even the humid night air couldn't slip between them and ran a finger down Marti's arm with slow deliberation.

"Maybe I need to put a collar on you."

Goddamn.

Marti didn't bother pretending she wasn't interested; they'd been through this dance before: sometimes quick and filthy against kitchen walls, sometimes drawn-out tension over cigarettes and stolen secrets.

"Then what are we waiting for?" she murmured, hooking two fingers into Pauline's belt loop and tugging her toward the pool house door.

The place loomed ahead: dark wood gleaming under artificial light, all sharp angles and sharp memories stretching into Thornfield's history of excesses.

The pool gurgled beside them as if whispering its own secrets into the night while moonlight splintered across its surface like broken glass.

Pauline grabbed the handle, turned back to wink at Marti, and stepped back. Marti let go of Pauline's belt loop and stepped inside first. "You didn't need a key?"

Pauline followed, flipping a light switch. "No lock. Just walk in."

Of course. Because nothing in this place made sense. The pool house was small but dressed up to look expensive; one of those designer attempts at minimalism that still screamed wealth. A single bed sat in the corner, sheets white enough to glow under artificial light, as if no one had ever dared sleep in it. A midnight-blue couch faced a sleek kitchenette: all stainless steel and polished surfaces untouched by real life. Across from it, a glass-walled shower stood waiting, frosted glass ghosting across its surface from the lingering heat of the day.

Marti pulled out her phone and started snapping pictures: bed, couch, kitchenette, shower. Then she began her search. Corners first, then under furniture, behind anything that could hide a camera or mic. No obvious bugs, but she pocketed two slip drives anyway. Evidence was evidence, even if she had no idea what was on them yet.

"You cleaned up since the cops were here," Marti said.

Pauline shrugged against the doorframe. "Not me. Mrs. Delacroix hired professionals. Spent an entire day scrubbing this place down."

Right. Scrubbed clean, like someone had something to hide. Nothing would be in plain sight if someone had gone through the place.

Marti hit the floor with a grunt, jeans catching on the edge of the carpet. She crawled toward the nightstand like a woman who'd done this before, which, depressingly, she had. Her fingers slid under the edge, hunting for something that didn't belong. Something wrong.

There. Rough tape against smooth wood. She peeled it back slowly, careful enough to make her nerves twitch. A small key fob dropped into her hand. No logo. No numbers. A matte black chunk of plastic heavy enough to feel like an accusation.

She turned it over in her palm and frowned. "What the fuck do you think this opens?"

Pauline leaned in from behind, her perfume sweet and sharp like guilt in a bottle. "Nothing in here," she said.

"Then why shove it up under your nightstand like a dirty secret?"

Pauline gave a half-shrug but didn't even try to answer. Typical.

Her knees couldn't take any more crawling. Marti pushed up off the floor and stalked over to the kitchenette like maybe it'd offer something less cryptic and more useful. She opened every cabinet twice: neat rows of dishes, too many wine glasses, crystal decanters lined up like they were waiting for inspection.

The last drawer stuck just enough to feel intentional, because of course it was.

She yanked harder and finally got it open.

Velvet jewelry roll tucked inside.

"No way," Marti muttered, rolling it out across the counter.

No jewelry. Of course not.

One memory card slipped free from a side pocket. In another, a stack of old-school rolled up photographs—actual printed photos—wrapped in a rubber band that had seen better days.

She pulled out the top photo and felt her stomach lurch sideways.

"Shit," she breathed.

Not because of who. It was Evelyn Delacroix, no surprise there. But Christ almighty, because of how.

Evelyn was splayed across an inflatable pool floaty in a position that screamed orgasm louder than any audio ever would—and it wasn't Thornfield between her thighs. It was Ari Stirling.

His face was right there: jaw tight, hair a mess from someone's hands, probably Evelyn's, and those storm-gray eyes locked on hers like they were mid-religious experience and forgot God existed outside each other's bodies.

Pauline leaned over her shoulder and hissed through her teeth. "Holy fuck."

"That's one word," Marti said flatly as she flipped through the rest of them fast enough to make her fingers hurt.

"Two. Learn to count," Pauline said.

Ari straddling Evelyn's hips.

Evelyn wrapping his tie around her own wrist.

A close-up where Evelyn stared dead into the camera mid-moan. Or mid-warning. It was hard to tell with lips parted like that and one eye half-lidded like she saw something no one else ever would again.

Marti almost missed the last piece, taped to the back of that final shot with cheap transparent scotch tape: a pale yellow sticky note with handwriting too elegant for this goddamned mess.

Never forget.

Well that was fucking ominous.

Footsteps outside pulled her attention back into high-alert mode. Too slow for security, too steady for someone harmless wandering late at night without purpose.

Marti shoved everything into her coat pocket in one smooth move and turned toward Pauline.

"Time to go."

Pauline didn't argue, just grabbed Marti's hand and followed her out into the garden shadows without hesitation or unnecessary words. They made it to Marti's car in record time, streetlight pooling gold across their escape route like spilled champagne no one got to drink.

The second they were in and doors shut, Pauline reached over with bold fingers trailing along Marti's chest like she already knew how this ended. "Quick fuck in the car?" she asked, voice all velvet filth and suggestion as she cupped Marti's breast through her jacket without shame or apology.

Marti caught Pauline's wrist and held it just long enough to say not yet, before leaning in anyway, brushing lips across cheekbone soft as regret but warmer than anything else tonight had given her.

"Another time," Marti murmured, voice low with want she wasn't about to indulge right now. "I've got bigger problems."

Pauline sighed theatrically but let go, falling back into her seat with a smirk that promised this wasn't over. Not by a long shot.

"Out."

Pauline got out of the car, pouted, stuck her tongue out, and slammed the door.

Stop teasing me with that tongue.

Marti drove home on autopilot, the hum of tires on wet pavement a poor distraction from the phantom pressure still ghosting over her skin. In bed, stretched bare against cool sheets, she let her fingers follow where Pauline's tongue had been just an hour earlier, chasing echoes of heat that refused to fade. She smirked at the ceiling as exhaustion pulled her under.

She barely noticed how long it had been since her last hit of Shadow.

Chapter 8

It was past midnight when Marti unlocked the office door. She shrugged off her soaked jacket and kicked off her wet boots at Lori's desk. Better here than tracking water into her own pit.

Marti dropped into her chair, reaching for the bottle of cheap whiskey and a dirty glass waiting for her. She thought about washing it but figured alcohol would kill bacteria. She threw back a shot, felt it burn, and poured another.

She flicked the disassembled taser glove across her desk, watching its exposed wiring spark before fizzling out. She needed to get it fixed, or maybe stop using it to short out vending machines.

She turned the slip drive over in her fingers, as if it might confess something before she plugged it in. Thornfield's data. His digital ghost. The whiskey bottle on her desk: cheap, rough, and half-empty since this morning, beckoned with the promise of forgetting.

She jammed the drive into her ancient computer and took a long pull from her glass. The burn hit fast, familiar. The system wheezed to life, a window blinking open with dozens of folders.

"Alright, Marcus," she muttered, cigarette hanging from her lips. "Let's see what kind of shit you were into."

The first folder: ACQUISITIONS-2054.

Contracts. Spreadsheets. Financial projections. Words blurred before snapping back into focus. She needed to concentrate; fresher cigarette, less booze clouding her brain. Snuffing out the current smoke in an overflowing ashtray, she lit another without thinking.

"Burger Baron... Crispy Chicken Shack... Happy Taco..." She scrolled, scanning file after file. "You weren't just dealing. You were cornering the goddamn fast food market."

People came in, walked out with closed bags and containers full of drugs instead of food: the perfect dealership.

The details of the stores were meticulous; buy failing restaurants for pennies, some renovation costs, and suddenly, success. With this system he was likely even writing off his initial stocking of any given restaurant.

Marti blinked and cocked her head. One name kept showing up where it didn't belong: Delacroix Holdings.

Marti snorted. "Well, well," she murmured. "Guess the grieving widow wasn't just crying into polyester sheets after all."

She clicked on an email thread dated three days before Thornfield ate a bullet: RE: Terms Unacceptable.

Thornfield's message was short and pissed-off: Your terms are highway robbery. I built this empire, not you. Back off or deal with the consequences.

Evelyn Delacroix didn't waste words either: You forget who financed your little burger adventure, Marcus. My family's money, my terms. Don't test me.

Marti exhaled smoke toward the ceiling, watching it curl like a thought she couldn't quite pin down. She clicked into another folder: PROJECTIONS.

Spreadsheets stacked deep with five-year forecasts for each restaurant he controlled, and plans to triple those holdings in two years flat.

She skimmed the numbers and smirked. No way these profits were just from fries and combo meals.

Her phone buzzed on the desk. Lori.

"Working?"

"Of course."

"Bullshit. Which alley are you bleeding out in? I'll come scrape you off the pavement," Lori laughed.

"You can come all you want. I'll watch. I'm at the office." Marti tilted her chair back, balancing a cigarette between two fingers. "Picked up some slip drives that might be useful."

"Picked up?"

"Mmm," was as committed as Marti was going to get.

A beat of silence. Then, "Anything good?"

"A bunch of fast food deals. Looks like Thornfield was the burger king. Dude knew what he was doing." She flicked through another file, hand drifting to the inside pocket of her jacket. The cool edge of her Shadow inhaler pressed against her palm like an old lover: familiar and dangerous.

The craving slammed into her. Shadow would clear the static in her brain, make sense of these numbers, help her see connections she might miss. Just one hit.

Liar.

Her fingers recoiled, curling into a fist as she reached for the whiskey instead. Different vice, same problem, more acceptability.

"You okay? You got quiet."

"I'm fine." Too sharp. She swallowed it down and tried again. "Just trying to piece this shit together. There are smarter ways, easier ways to launder drug money."

Lori made a thoughtful noise on the other end of the line. "Maybe check any other folders?"

Marti opened "CORRESPONDENCE" and wished she hadn't. Thousands of emails flooded the screen like an avalanche of corporate bullshit.

"Oh, fuck no," she muttered. "This shit is your problem now."

"Nice," Lori huffed. "I'm almost there."

Good enough for Marti. She hung up, put feet on the desk, whiskey warming a slow burn in her throat as she eyed the second slip drive sitting next to the bottle. Her fingers twitched toward her pocket again, as if addiction had hardwired itself into her bones. The office door swung open before she could linger.

"Honey! I'm home!"

Marti exhaled through barely parted lips as Lori stepped inside: soaked from head to toe, rain trailing down bare arms, jeans clinging to every inch of something Marti tried not to stare at. And failed at doing so.

"Come get it," Marti said without thinking, or maybe with too much thinking, and when Lori moved toward her, still dripping and smug about it, Marti groaned in her throat before she could bite it back.

Lori froze mid-step. "Did you just—?"

"Fuck yes," Marti muttered, pouring another two fingers of whiskey and knocking it back in one go just to give herself something else to focus on that wasn't Lori's everything right now. The whiskey didn't do nearly enough to chase away what she really wanted beneath her skin.

Lori smirked but let it slide for now and nodded toward the computer screen, glancing over Marti's mess of files and drives scattered across the desk as if a crime scene waiting for a detective with patience she didn't have.

"You going through all this?"

"Not anymore." Marti shoved one slip drive vaguely in Lori's direction; this was secretary work and not the kind of puzzle-solving she cared about right now. She grabbed her coat, heading for the door before regret could talk her out of this plan.

"I'm hitting Thornfield's office in person," she said over her shoulder as she palmed another cigarette.

Lori caught the drive with one hand but didn't look happy about it. "Be careful."

Marti patted her shoulder holster and shot Lori a grin that had no business being as cocky as it was reckless.

"When am I not?"

She left before Lori could answer, not because she didn't want to hear it but because she knew what she'd say. She lit up as soon as she stepped into the damp night air.

Rain slicked down the pavement outside as Delacroix's final emails played in her mind: Back off or deal with the consequences.

She wondered if those consequences had caught up to him.

And if they were about to catch up to her next.

Falls City spread before Marti like an open wound: slick streets glistening under neon light, rain pooling in broken asphalt as garbage choked the gutters. The air here clung thick with exhaust and desperation, pressing against her ribs with each breath. This was where people came to disappear, or be disappeared if they weren't careful.

She inhaled deep, lungs protesting like they did now. She pulled out her inhaler and took a hit to steady herself. Good enough for now.

A rustling in the alleyway sent tension curling up her spine; her hand darted toward the gun at her hip before she heard it: a voice slithering through the dark like oil over water.

"You lost?"

Marti turned, weight shifting onto one foot as she sized him up: a wiry man leaning against crumbling brick, sharp features cut deeper by flickering lights nearby. His grin was too easy. His eyes said he was calculating how much trouble she'd be if he pushed his luck.

"Mind your fucking business," she said. She pulled the gun halfway out of the holster.

He chuckled but didn't press further, melting back into shadow as if he'd never been there.

Marti exhaled through gritted teeth, nestled her gun, and kept moving. The city pressed tight around her as she wove through abandoned warehouses and boarded-up storefronts whose walls whispered old secrets if you knew how to listen. Past broken glass and forgotten alleyways was what she needed: Thornfield's kingdom.

A perfect hideout for someone who thought himself untouchable.

Her boots echoed off wet pavement as she walked deeper into Falls City's rotting core. Something coiled at the edges of awareness as if unseen eyes tracked every step she took, but Marti didn't flinch.

Let them watch.

The tower rose out of the city's filth like a knife in an open wound: sharp, cold, and humming with the kind of power that didn't bother pretending it gave a damn. It was Thornfield's monument to himself, a concrete monolith soaked in neon reflections and dirty money. The place reeked of control. Secrets stacked so high they pressed against the tinted windows, desperate to crawl free.

How tall is that fucking thing?

Marti wanted those secrets, and had Evelyn Delacroix's permission to talk.

Marti lit another cigarette and took a drag, eyeing the building as if it might bite. It probably would. Past those pristine glass doors was a world where power didn't just corrupt; it devoured. The kind of place where deals were made with the quiet weight of a handshake, where people disappeared without a trace, and where every smile hid teeth eager for flesh.

She crushed the cigarette under her heel and pushed forward.

Security wrapped around the lobby like a noose: tight, suffocating, ready to snap shut the second someone twitched wrong. Guards in crisp uniforms watched her with expressions just shy of unrestrained ferocity, their hands close enough to their weapons to make a point. Metal detectors stood like sentinels, waiting to strip away any illusions of privacy.

Way more security for the suits than the grieving widow.

Marti stepped through the doors and kept her face blank as one of the guards swept his gaze down her body as if trying to see past skin, muscle, bone, to whatever secrets she might be carrying beneath them.

"Marti Starova," she said when she reached the receptionist's desk. The guy didn't even blink at her name, just kept typing like he had all the time in the world.

"Mrs. Delacroix said I could speak with Mr. Thornfield's staff," she added when he still didn't look up. The truth. For once.

There was a soft hum as the receptionist clicked something on his screen. "Look here."

Marti lifted her head just in time for the flash of a camera: too fast to stop it, too late to hide from its gaze. A printer whirred beside him, spitting out a plastic badge with her face on it, a terrible fucking photo that made her look half-dead and pissed about it. He looped it onto a lanyard and slid it across the counter toward her.

"Always keep it on," he said. "Unless you feel like getting shot."

A buzzer sounded behind her, metal detector calling out something it didn't like, and she held back an eye-roll as she turned toward the nearest guard. She handed over her gun first, then fished out her inhalers before they could start asking stupid questions about them too.

A nod pointed her toward the elevators, the kind that moved smooth and silent like they had nothing to prove, and every inch of Marti rebelled at stepping inside that metal tomb waiting to swallow her whole.

Fuck this part of the job.

The doors slid shut behind her, sealing her into its sleek walls with a faint hiss as air got thinner, colder, pressing in too tight all at once. Her hand wrapped around the lanyard instead of reaching for another cigarette, gripping hard enough that creases bit into plastic and skin alike as she forced herself still while gravity pulled at every inch of her bones.

Too fast. Too fucking fast. The elevator surged upward as if it had somewhere better to be than carrying dead weight through Thornfield's kingdom, dragging Marti with it whether she liked it or not. The city blurred beyond dark glass as floors zipped past in flashes of distant light and movement, none of it real enough to anchor herself to anything except the rapid thud-thud-thud hammering against her ribs.

She swallowed against bile crawling up her throat and locked her knees before they gave out beneath her; she wouldn't let Thornfield's fortress see her crack before she even reached its heart.

The doors slid open with a muted chime, and Marti stumbled out, legs unsteady, gut twisting. The weight in her chest loosened, just a little, but the ghost of it clung like cigarette smoke in old fabric.

Chapter 9

"Who the fuck are you?"

The voice hit before she could steady herself. A wall of uniform and muscle stepped into her path: a security grunt built like a battering ram, close-cropped hair bristling under the fluorescents. His meaty hand shot out, snatching at her lanyard as if it was made of gold.

Marti didn't flinch. She was doing everything she could not to puke on his shoes. She was no fan of elevators.

Meat Wall stood there while he squinted at the pass as if it might morph into something more believable if he stared hard enough. Silence stretched between them, thick as the cravings scratching at the back of her skull. For one long second, she thought he'd toss her back onto the elevator, maybe straight through the doors without opening them first.

Then: a grunt, low and reluctant. He let go.

Marti rolled her shoulder as she stepped past him, fingers drifting over where his grip had lingered too long. Asshole. The marble floors beneath her boots gleamed with money, reflecting cold artificial light as she moved toward reception.

Frances, or so her name plate claimed, was waiting, poised behind a sleek desk with an air that managed to be both regal and unimpressed. Silver hair sharp as a blade, blazer crisp enough to cut glass. The kind of woman who'd seen enough bullshit for three lifetimes and wasn't about to put up with any more for free.

Marti flashed something that might have been a smile if you were feeling generous. "Marti Starova. I have questions about Marcus Thornfield."

Frances studied her like one might study an insect they weren't sure was venomous yet. Then: "I will not speak ill of the dead."

Marti let the words hang between them for a beat before knocking them aside like cigarette ash off cheap fabric. "Mrs. Delacroix cleared me to ask." A pause, then: "I'm investigating his death. At Ari Stirling's request."

She had no more names to drop, but that last one got Frances' attention; not much, but enough for her gaze to flicker somewhere distant before returning sharp and clear as ever. "Mr. Thornfield was... complicated." Polite phrasing for 'absolute nightmare,' if Marti had to guess. "Charming when it suited him, volatile when it didn't."

"Volatile how?"

A slight purse of lips, as if Frances was weighing whether this counted as talking shit about the dead or just telling inconvenient truths. "He yelled," she admitted. "Threw things sometimes."

Marti's pen scratched against paper in short, deliberate strokes, capturing every shift in tone, every quiet refusal to elaborate further than necessary. "Anyone piss him off more than usual?"

Frances gave her a look so dry it could've turned wine back into grapes. "Language," she chided before continuing, "If you're looking for someone who endured Mr. Thornfield's temper most often... Viktor Ivanov comes to mind." A slow exhale through her nose. Something almost amused in her voice now. "Those two went at it more than once every day."

"Which way?"

Frances flicked a wrist to the left and smirked. Marti filed that away under interesting and offered Frances a nod before turning on her heel toward Ivanov's office. If Thornfield had made someone's life hell on a regular basis, that someone might have had motive to return the favor permanently.

The hallway narrowed around her as she moved deeper into it. The concrete tower pressed close again now that distraction had passed. Shadows stretched long under dim fluorescents buzzing overhead like dying insects trapped behind glass.

More name plates, these ones on doors. Mathew Reynolds, Isabelle Webb, Lorenzo Bradford, Colby Whitehead.

She knocked twice on Viktor Ivanov's door, not tentative, not polite, then pushed it open without waiting for permission because fuck permission.

Inside: opulence dripping from every surface. Dark wood gleamed under soft amber light, leather seating pristine enough to make someone hesitate before actually using it. A room meant to project power; or perhaps to hide insecurity under expensive polish.

Interesting contrast to the rest of this place, as if someone wanted visitors to know exactly who held the real leash around here.

Viktor barely glanced up. Sharp, wiry, more rat-like than Rat. Fingers drumming against polished wood, impatience carved into every precise movement. He didn't offer a greeting. Didn't need to.

"Mr. Ivanov."

"I know who you are and what you want," he cut in, flicking his gaze toward her before dismissing her just as fast. "Frances called ahead, doing her job, you know."

Marti dropped into the chair across from him without waiting for an invitation. "Then let's not waste time. How's business?"

"Profitable." A bored answer. "And yours?"

"I'm at the part where I ask the questions," she said. "Tell me about Marcus Thornfield."

Viktor's nose wrinkled as if she'd put something rotten on his expensive carpet. "A scandalous man, Ms. Starova," he said, voice clipped with distaste. "Brought women into his office like it was his personal brothel. Closed the blinds when he remembered to care who saw." A sneer curled at his mouth. "Sometimes didn't bother."

Marti leaned forward, elbows on her knees. "Anyone in particular? A habit or just bad impulse control?"

"I don't keep track of the man's conquests," Viktor said with a dismissive wave of his hand. "He split his time between here and home. His maid might have more insight than me. Don't bother his poor widow. He bragged about the maid."

The words landed sharp and cold in Marti's gut: not some vague rumor or whispered assumption but something solid. Her pulse spiked though she kept her expression flat, unreadable.

"His maid." She forced the words out evenly, as if they didn't come with a kick to the ribs.

Viktor nodded once, crisp and final. "No boundaries, no decency," he said, like that covered everything that needed saying about Marcus Thornfield's character. And maybe it did.

Pauline's face burned behind Marti's eyes: sweet, sexy Pauline with her teasing smile and soft hands resting against Marti's flesh. Shit. Fucking shit.

She'd said nothing.

Marti swallowed down the sudden acidic sting at the back of her throat and stood too fast, biting out something that might have been thanks before stalking out of Viktor's office.

The hallway stretched long ahead of her, fluorescent light humming above as if static filled her skull as she forced one foot in front of the other toward the elevator at the end of the hall. Her hands curled into fists at her sides because of course Pauline hadn't said anything; this was how it always went when Marti let someone close enough to matter.

Fucking rabbit holes leading from one place to another right back to the fucking beginning.

The elevator doors slid open with their mechanical groan, and she stepped inside even though every muscle screamed against it. She hated this fucking metal box with its stale air and its slow descent down twenty-three floors, like a goddamn coffin lowering into the ground.

She clenched her jaw as she rode it down, breath shallow, as if taking too deep a drag of air would press heavier against her ribs. By the time she hit street level she was reaching for Shadow.

One quick inhale scorched down her throat. Just one. But enough to dull something. Not everything. Not close.

Fingers trembling around her phone as she stabbed Pauline's number into the keypad.

Voicemail.

Of course.

Her voice came out rough when she spoke, seething as anger tangled with betrayal: "How long were you planning on keeping this from me?" A slow inhale through gritted teeth before she continued, steady but sharp as a knife pressed to skin: "Call me back."

Marti's tires screamed against pavement as she swerved onto the narrow road leading to the Delacroix mansion, one hand locked around the wheel, the other shaking from too much Shadow or not enough. The house loomed ahead like some gothic nightmare, all sharp shadows and cold stone. Marti was already halfway out of the car before it stopped. The door slammed shut behind her.

Feet pounding up the steps. Fist hammering against polished wood.

"Pauline!" Her voice rang sharp, slicing through the quiet. "Open the goddamn door!"

A hesitant pause. Then footsteps. The lock clicked.

Pauline appeared in the doorway, wide-eyed and barefoot, one strap of her tank top sliding off a shoulder as if she'd been dragged out of sleep. "Jesus, Marti," she muttered, squinting against the porch light. "Stop shouting or you'll piss off Mrs. Delacroix. Even more than you already have."

Marti shoved forward until they were chest to chest, heat rolling off her skin in waves of fury held together by nicotine and sheer fucking willpower. "You lied to me." No preamble. No buildup. Just that raw edge of betrayal scraping its way out of her throat. "You let me stand there like an idiot while Ivanov told me about you and Thornfield."

Pauline blinked once, slow, then snorted: fucking snorted, as if this was funny. She planted a hand on Marti's chest and pushed her back just enough to breathe. "That what this is about?" A smirk ghosted across her lips, lazy and amused in a way that made Marti want to kiss her or punch a hole through something expensive just to break it off her face. "You think I fucked Thornfield?" She let that hang there for a second before tilting her head, voice dipping low: "Marti, I don't do dick."

That should've been relief slamming into Marti's ribs instead of more frustration, but her brain hadn't caught up with her pulse yet. "Then explain why Viktor Ivanov said to ask Thornfield's maid?"

Pauline rolled her eyes but didn't step back, didn't let go of where her fingers still pressed against Marti's sternum. "Giselle," she said. "The other maid. The one bending over backwards for Thornfield: literally."

Marti clenched her teeth so hard a headache bloomed behind one eye. Fucking Ivanov and his half-assed statement. "You're sure?"

Instead of answering, Pauline let her hand trail downward, slow drag of fingertips over fabric, until they hit bare skin above Marti's waistband. Fingers pressing just enough to make Marti shift on instinct before she caught herself, stiffening with a glare that did nothing to stop whatever game Pauline thought she was playing.

"You're jealous," Pauline murmured, mouth curling at the edges as if she'd figured out something important despite how obvious it was.

"Apparently," Marti muttered.

A soft laugh as Pauline traced something: a heart? over the front of Marti's shirt with one finger before shifting closer, sliding an arm around Marti's waist like she had every right to touch her however she wanted. Her thumb brushed over fabric where it clung tight across Marti's chest, teasing at something close to smug satisfaction.

"Don't fuck with me," Marti warned.

"I'll fuck with you plenty," Pauline shot back without pause, voice dipping suggestive before snapping back to business: "After I prove my alibi. I know how this works."

One hand sliding free from where it had settled low on Marti's spine as she pulled out her phone from a back pocket. She tapped at the screen once before holding it up between them: two digital movie tickets glowing in the low light, both with names attached.

"Me and Giselle," Pauline said. "At the movies. Same night Thornfield shot himself."

"Giselle?"

"His maid. And lover."

"Did Evelyn know?"

Pauline threw her head back and laughed. "She demanded it. She and Marcus gave up sexual relations a while ago. I don't know why or when. But Giselle told me Marcus is into some kinky shit."

"Sounds like the kind of man I'd drink a whiskey with."

Pauline grinned. "You're a complex woman," she murmured.

"I'm so complex even I don't know how I feel," Marti admitted.

Pauline hummed at that answer, somewhere between pleased and intrigued, and leaned in just enough for breath to ghost over Marti's jaw when she spoke next:

"Well... whatever you feel? It makes me wet."

Pauline's lips found Marti's, slow at first, testing, then insistent. Marti answered in kind, hands slipping beneath Pauline's shirt, dragging her closer. Heat built between them, breathless and demanding, until the world outside the Delacroix mansion ceased to exist.

When they finally broke apart, Marti let out a shaky exhale, her pulse hammering beneath her skin. She should've felt something clean and simple: relief, maybe. Instead, it tangled with something messier, something that made her want to pull Pauline back in and say fuck it to everything else.

Pauline traced a finger down Marti's jaw, amusement flickering in her gaze. "Now go be a PI." A kiss to her temple. "Find out who killed Thornfield." Another, softer this time. "And don't get that pretty face of yours wrecked in the process."

Marti would've laughed if she weren't already backing away, if she didn't think staying another second would make leaving impossible.

Pauline lingered in the doorway as Marti slid behind the wheel and started the engine. "Be careful," she called, before shutting the door between them.

Why was everyone saying that?

Marti retreated to her car but stayed parked in the driveway, refusing to leave until she had it figured out. Evelyn had no security detail (for reasons that made Marti suspicious), but she took advantage, staying right where she was.

And thought.

Ari Stirling had motive; the only way to become king is to kill the king. What gnawed at her wasn't why he wanted Thornfield gone. It was why he'd dragged her into this mess when he could've let it all rot under police incompetence instead. Hiring a PI didn't track, not unless there was something more to bury under all that wealth and power than just one dead body.

Her fingers drummed against the wheel as she turned over every angle in her head, as if she were certain she was missing something obvious but couldn't see it through all the flashing neon distractions of greed and deception littering her path like broken glass.

She pulled out her smart-paper pad, flipping through the pages of scrawled notes. Eveyln Delacroix, who threatened him but seemed legitimately widowy. Viktor Ivanov, VP of Finance: disgusted by Thornfield, but disgust wasn't murder. Colin Bonner, the health inspector drowning in bribes, but how would Thornfield's death help him? Frances, the tight-lipped receptionist who knew more than she let on. And now Giselle, the maid tangled in Thornfield's sheets.

Her phone buzzed. Lori texting her a news alert. Mayor Bruce Garrison (that piece of shit could be included on the suspect list) speaking at what should have been a somber memorial for Thornfield. Marti tapped play and watched, her eyes narrowing as the mayor's composed face filled the screen.

"My fellow citizens, today we remember Marcus Thornfield, whose passing has impacted our community. While we often stood on opposite sides politically, his contributions, especially to downtown revitalization and our public library, leave a lasting legacy."

Jesus Christ, politicians.

"Beyond politics, Marcus was a man of quiet generosity, and his kindness touched many lives. As we mourn, let's support his family and honor the good he did. My deepest condolences to the Thornfield and Delacroix families; may his legacy endure."

Marti's jaw tightened. The careful phrasing, the strategic pauses. This was calculated to control the damage from his earlier rant. Garrison was too skilled a politician to risk his reputation with that shit.

She tapped her stylus against the steering wheel. Her gaze drifted back to Evelyn's mansion. The widow would have something to say.

She stubbed out her cigarette with force.

Yeah.

She needed to talk to Evelyn.

And she needed to do it now.

"Mrs. Delacroix, I appreciate you seeing me again." Marti settled into the antique chair across from Evelyn, who looked composed in a tailored black dress that cost more than Marti's monthly rent.

"I told you, Ms. Starova. Call me Evelyn." She offered a smile that didn't reach her eyes. "Pauline said you had vital questions. What do you need from me today?"

Marti cut straight to it. "Mayor Garrison seems to think your husband was involved in corruption, that his philanthropy was a cover for manipulation."

Something flickered across Evelyn's face; so brief Marti almost missed it. Not anger. Not amusement. Recognition.

"Bruce Garrison," Evelyn said the name as if it was something unpleasant on the bottom of her shoe, "has been over to see Marcus dozens of times. They talk politics, they talk business. Bruce talked crap about my husband. I saw the video. Now... well, I did not go to his memorial for my husband. But I watched the broadcast. Bruce is distasteful."

"He said there would be a lasting legacy."

Evelyn took a sip from her teacup. "That's a new low, even for Bruce. He's working to tear apart everything Marcus created: the library, the new wing in the hospital. All of it."

"Any idea what's going on? Overhear any of their conversation?"

Evelyn set down her cup with a clink against the saucer. "I made it my business to stay out of my husband's business."

A pause. Just a heartbeat too long. "Perhaps." Evelyn's voice was measured. "Marcus knew Bruce better than most people realized."

Marti leaned forward. "What exactly do you mean by 'knew him better than most'?"

Evelyn sighed. "Bruce Garrison crafts his public image with the precision of a diamond cutter. Every word, every gesture calculated for maximum political effect. But in private?" She shrugged. "Let's just say the mayor's personal interests don't always align with his political platform."

"That's cryptic."

"It's meant to be." Evelyn stood, signaling the end of their conversation. "I have nothing more for you, Ms. Starova."

"Can I access information about the library and hospital projects?" Marti stood as well. "Where would I find those?"

"I believe he kept most of his records at his downtown office." Evelyn walked to a small writing desk and scribbled something on a card. "Show this to Frances. She'll give you access."

Marti took the card, noting the elegant script. "Thank you."

"Don't thank me yet." Evelyn's eyes were hard, the socialite veneer cracking just enough to show steel beneath.

"Marcus valued privacy, his own and others'. Whatever you find, remember that not all secrets deserve to be exposed. Get out." Evelyn didn't bother waiting for Marti to leave before pulling out a golden inhaler. So much for not being addictive.

Back to that hellhole.

* * *

Frances met her at the elevator, keys in hand.

"Mrs. Delacroix called ahead," she said, her manner unchanged from their previous meeting. "Follow me."

The office was immaculate, cleaned since Thornfield's death but otherwise untouched. Frances led her to a walnut desk that cost more than Marti's car. Which honestly was pretty easy.

"His philanthropic files are in the cabinet behind the desk. The community project materials should be in the third drawer." Frances hesitated. "Will you need anything else?"

"No," Marti said. "Thanks."

Frances nodded and left, closing the door behind her.

Marti went straight for the drawer, finding a neat folder labeled "East Falls Development." Inside were architectural renderings, budget proposals, and correspondence. She flipped through them, looking for anything connecting to Garrison.

A small envelope slipped from between two pages, landing on the desktop with a soft whisper. Marti's fingers hesitated before opening it; these moments felt like crossing a threshold, as if she was about to learn something she couldn't un-know.

Inside was a photograph: Thornfield at what appeared to be a private fundraiser, champagne flute in hand, mid-laugh. But it was the background that made her breath catch. Garrison stood half-hidden behind a column, watching Thornfield with an expression that felt obscene in its nakedness: desire mixed with something darker, more possessive. The mayor's public mask had slipped completely.

She turned the photo over. Written in a precise, measured hand: Bruce: Remember where we started. This center means everything. Don't let politics destroy what matters.

Marti set the photo down, struck by the intimacy of the message. This wasn't some corporate rival sending a professional warning. This was personal: a reminder of shared history, of something meaningful between them.

Her phone buzzed against the desk. Lori: Mayor G's speech from earlier is exploding online. Check the comments section. People are connecting dots.

Marti pulled up the video, scrolling past the predictable partisan flames. Then one comment stopped her cold. Username @TruthTeller28: The mayor doth protest too much. Three separate nights at the Skyline Hotel last month, same night Thornfield's car was there. No security detail. No record of meetings. #HiddenAgenda

She flipped back to the photo, studying it with fresh eyes. Garrison's gaze held something beyond mere observation: a proprietary intensity that made her skin prickle.

"Son of a bitch," she muttered, pieces clicking into place.

She needed to visit the Baker Center. If there was anyone who knew the truth about Falls City's closeted elite, it would be the veterans of the LGBTQ community center. Those queens had all the secrets.

Her phone buzzed again as she slipped the photo into her pocket. Lori: Mayor just announced emergency press conference tomorrow. Proposing legislation to ban Pride flags on city property. Called it "anti-divisiveness initiative." Fucking hypocrite.

Marti paused, her hand still on the drawer. The timeline was accelerating. Garrison wasn't just hiding who he was; he was actively destroying it. And people who destroy their shadow lives often destroy other lives too.

She closed the drawer with a soft click. Falls City's upstanding mayor had just moved to the top of her suspect list.

Chapter 10

The rain was relentless, stabbing Falls City with a thousand tiny daggers. Marti huddled under the flimsy canopy of an abandoned storefront, swearing as her boots filled with cold, dirty water. The streets shimmered with oily puddles reflecting the neon glow, blurring the line between filth and the night sky. She glanced at her phone again, her fingers twitching as the screen lit up.

A message from Lori: We have proof of Garrison and Thornfield. Slip drive.

"Fuck," Marti muttered, biting her lip hard enough to draw blood. What had she missed?

She turned towards the office, trying to clear her mind, to shake off the suffocating grip of Shadow. She'd almost forgotten about the slip drives she'd swiped from the pool house. Proof that she was no longer the law-abiding detective she once was. Marti started running.

Her heart thundered in her chest as she dashed across streets, dodging cars that barely noticed her presence. Each beat reminded her she was human, limited. The familiar outline of her second home loomed ahead, a sanctuary in a city that had forgotten what it meant to care.

The office door creaked open, and Marti stumbled inside, her guts aching from the sprint. Struggling for breath, she lit a cigarette, the smoke a comfort in the chaos.

"Jesus, Marti, you can barely breathe as it is. Put that damned thing out," Lori growled, looking up from her desk.

Marti glanced at the cigarette, then snuffed it out on the carpet with a defiant grin.

"What the hell, woman? This is a rental suite!" Lori snapped.

"Not my best morning, okay? That tribute to Thornfield, and then Evelyn and... And now there were videos in all that data?"

"Surprise fucking surprise. It was on the slip drive you gave me, not the one you looked at. Come here. I've got something you need to see." Lori tapped her computer screen, her eyes bright with something beyond exhaustion. "Look at this jackpot. It's Garrison. Videos."

Marti raised a skeptical eyebrow but moved closer, drawn by the urgency in Lori's gaze. On the screen, Thornfield writhed in pleasure, exposed in a way that screamed scandal. Her fingers left smudges as she swiped through the evidence.

"Big deal. Lots of people take it up the ass," Marti scoffed, turning away to sink into the guest chair.

"You stopped before the real shit," Lori said, tapping a few more times. "Get over here, take a look at this."

Marti rolled her eyes but couldn't ignore the pull. She stood, sauntered over, and looked.

The room seemed to close in as she stared at the screen. Garrison: the self-righteous mayor of Falls City, entangled with Marcus Thornfield, lost in a moment of raw, forbidden passion. This was a bombshell that could fracture the city's power balance. It would tear down Garrison's carefully built facade and plunge the investigation into chaos.

"Jesus," Marti muttered, her pulse quickening as she flicked through the photos, each one more incriminating than the last. "No wonder he's been so shady. It's him and Thornfield."

"Exactly," Lori said, her voice tight with the kind of thrill Marti knew would later bite them both in the ass. "This is it, Marti. We've got the mayor by the balls."

Marti exhaled, leaning against the edge of her desk. "Balls and dick, kid. Don't forget the dick." She kept her tone light, sharp, but her brain was spinning. The files laid out a filthy little narrative she couldn't ignore: Mayor Garrison, moral crusader and public darling, on his knees for Thornfield, Falls City's favorite dead drug lord. The story had everything: sleaze, power, secrets big enough to shatter careers into ash.

"Does it even matter?" Lori asked, cutting through her thoughts like a knife.

"It's motive." Marti's eyes narrowed, the weight of it all pressing down. She dragged on her cigarette and let the smoke curl out. "But not if we make the wrong move. Garrison's already working overtime covering his tracks. Stirring up the dust, throwing shade everywhere. If we're not careful, we'll choke on it."

Marti pushed off the desk and wandered towards the couch, her space filled with the sticky sweet staleness of too many cigarettes and not enough windows cracked open. Lori followed, the quiet clack of her heels soft against the hardwood. Marti collapsed onto the couch, boot heels thudding against the armrest as she swung her feet up. "We've got him railing Thornfield, condemning queers in public, and declaring the man's death a murder." She tapped her ash into the tray. "It's all on file."

"Yeah," Lori said, standing over her. Determination drove a sharp line between her brows, her green eyes burning. "But we know that connection runs deep, right? And he said Thornfield was killed. It's officially on record. Not a suicide."

"Save the files to the server. Garrison folder." Marti's voice was clipped as her mind raced ahead. "We confirm it's legit. Here's what I think happened: Thornfield filmed it all; not just Garrison, but the others, too. Blackmail, it must be. If he had a mayor screwing him, imagine who else he had. Murder, blackmail, leverage: it's always about power. But I need to see every video. Everything."

Lori hesitated, biting her lip. "There's a lot to go through," she admitted. "And Thornfield didn't just film Garrison. He filmed himself with... a lot of people." Her tone shifted under the weight of what they had stumbled into. "Okay, but once we've got that, then what?"

"Then the suspect list grows." Marti's gaze hardened. "Garrison's got company, but we're not playing guess-the-perp just yet. First, we get names for these faces."

Lori nodded. "Files will be secure in a few minutes. You need anything else from me?"

"Privacy," Marti said, letting a low laugh slip as she eased herself back up from the couch. It was thin, brittle; everything between them was emotion spread too thin over a growing expanse of danger. She crossed to her door and shut it behind her, leaving Lori in the hush of the outer office.

Inside the quiet, the footage swallowed the room. Marti lit another cigarette, the ember glowing as she fast-forwarded through Thornfield's greatest hits. Frame after frame, her sharp eyes scanned every grainy face, every bare shoulder. Searching.

Pauline wouldn't be there. Pauline couldn't be there. That's what she told herself over and over again. But the little seed of doubt, planted in the wreckage of Marti's heart, kept growing. She kinda liked the woman.

Still, the footage rolled on. Garrison, grunting under Thornfield's weight. Knees on the floor, face slack. The video quality was shit: blurry, flickering, but the raw intimacy of it seeped through, inescapable. Thornfield leaned in, whispering something Marti couldn't hear, and Garrison's body trembled. Marti leaned into the screen, transfixed, the heat crawling up her neck against her will.

Somewhere between one breath and the next, her hand dropped to her lap. She hated herself for it. Not really. She didn't stop. Not yet.

The thought of Lori walking in on her mid-orgasm sent one last shiver down Marti's spine. Her body tightened, released, and stilled, the blood pounding in her temples receding just enough for her to hear something beyond her own ragged breathing.

She slumped back in the chair, sticky discomfort already making itself known, before lazily pulling her hand from where it shouldn't have been. She studied her glistening fingers for one beat, then licked them clean. Napkin. Desk. Wipe. Same dance, different tune.

Pants up. Cigarette lit. Business as usual.

For someone who spent her days watching other people fuck, armed with a half-dead sense of purpose and working on the clock, she was starting to think about hiring someone to knock Shadow out of her system permanently. The late-night binge wasn't helping. She hit play on the next video but dragged the cursor along the timeline, her face cold and bored despite the nudity flashing across the screen.

If Pauline's face had shown up, Marti wasn't sure she'd have made it through without gagging or throwing something. Thankfully, it didn't. A relief, albeit small, considering the sheer volume of dirt on the hard drive. Over twenty videos recorded over three months. Four different men. Four potential suspects. Marti spun her chair away from the screen with a grunt, ignoring the faces still burned into her head.

"Nightmare," she muttered to herself.

The knock came without warning, though Lori never waited to be invited in. As if the woman hadn't already crossed all kinds of thresholds; what was another door between them? Marti clicked to close the image she'd stopped on and exhaled enough smoke to blur the air between them.

Lori glanced at the cigarette but said nothing, standing close enough for Marti to catch her clean, lemony scent cutting through the room's musk.

"Got a minute?" Lori asked, the tone deliberate.

"What do you want?" Marti answered through a line of smoke, not bothering to make it sound like she cared.

Lori, leaning against the desk as if she owned it, pointed a slender finger at the top of Marti's screen, tapping twice on the link she'd just sent. Her sweet, sultry mouth broke into something close to a smirk. "Our boy Garrison? He's a regular at The Handsome Dove. Like, daily regular. Thought you might care."

Marti took another drag, slow and thoughtful, before blowing it straight toward the ceiling. "Garrison at a club for assholes? Didn't pin him as someone that subtle."

"Maybe he's less subtle after a few drinks," Lori said, arms folded but with that glimmer in her eye Marti didn't trust. "Could be worth having a chat over a whiskey or three."

Marti tapped ash into the overfull tray at her elbow. "Sure. Butter him up. Buy him a round. See if he can talk and hold his liquor at the same time."

"And if he can't?"

Marti shrugged, the corner of her mouth twitching. "It's not like I'm above taking notes on drunk confessions. Who knows what he'd spill if we play the pity angle: nobody appreciates him, big man carrying the weight of the world on his shoulders, blah blah blah."

Lori tilted her head. "You think he's tied to more than just screwing Thornfield?"

Marti frowned and stubbed her cigarette out. "What did we say about corrupt people getting handsy with bigger criminals? Politicians, drug bosses; Falls City loves its little crossovers. Remember Jameson? Getting head under his desk during a call with the President?"

Lori grimaced but didn't argue. "Fair point."

Marti lit another cigarette. "The Handsome Dove it is. Just make sure he's drunk enough to slip up before they cut us off."

"Yeah, he went on about being the victim of the biggest, ugliest smear campaign this city had ever seen," Lori said, leaning back in her chair. "He kept saying his enemies were trying to destroy the 'greatest moment in Falls City's history.' Apparently, that involves talking to the President, because sure, why not."

"And it worked. The guy got reelected," Marti said, flicking ash into the overflowing tray on her desk. "Falls City forgives a hell of a lot of crap."

"God knows it forgets even more," Lori said.

"If it were just sex with Thornfield, this guy could play the tragic victim. 'Oh no, I was coerced, manipulated, blackmailed.' The voters would eat that shit up." Marti flicked ash into the tray overflowing with cigarette butts. "But there's more. There's always more. We just need him to open up."

She leaned back in her chair, staring out at the rain streaking down the grimy window. Smoke curled around her fingers as she tapped her cigarette against the edge of the tray. The night outside felt thick, waiting.

Then it hit her. She sat up, making the chair creak. "I've got it."

Lying to a suspect had never been an option when she was a homicide detective: ethics, policies, the whole goddamn rulebook weighing her down. But now? Now she could do whatever she wanted.

"If Thornfield filmed these encounters, who's to say the camera wasn't rolling that night too?"

Lori frowned. "We don't have that footage."

"Garrison doesn't know that." Marti took another drag, exhaled. "We won't accuse him outright; we don't have enough for that yet. But if we just happen to run into him, casually drop that we've got footage we haven't reviewed yet…" She shrugged. "If he panics? That tells us everything we need to know."

Lori narrowed her eyes. "So we lie?"

Marti gasped and clutched at imaginary pearls as if she were some scandalized socialite. Lori swatted her upside the head.

"We take it slow," Marti said, grinning through the sting of Lori's palm. "See what shakes loose." She stood and grabbed her coat from where it hung over the back of her chair. "Let's head to The Handsome Dove."

"I'll grab NeuroLocks," Lori said, already on her feet. She disappeared into the office's tiny, dimly lit closet, the door creaking on its hinges. It looked like a junkie's dream in there, or maybe a black-market pharmacy. Shelves stacked with contraband medical supplies sagged under their weight, shadows pooling in the corners like secrets.

The faint whine of aging tech mingled with the acrid, sterile tang of antiseptic, and Lori's fingers skimmed over a lineup of vials and injectors. NeuroLock: a twenty-four-hour fix to keep the hazy grip of MethLumina, the latest drug of choice, from messing up your head. Right next to it, ViaRevive, packed in delicate glass vials that promised to stitch up gunshot wounds or busted ribs in minutes. A shiny slab of SynthoSkin caught the low light, printed flesh ready to replace whatever piece of you had been torn away. It was like staring at an inventory for surviving how badly Falls City wanted you dead.

"God, we've got half a hospital in here," Marti muttered, leaning against the doorframe, watching Lori rummage.

Lori pulled out two vials of NeuroLock and their matching injectors. "Well, if you stopped getting shot for five goddamn minutes, we wouldn't need all this," she said as she loaded an injector. "This stash would cost a fortune if we went through legitimate channels."

"Wouldn't be Falls City if it came easy," Marti said. She winced as Lori slammed the injector into her neck without warning. The NeuroLock flooded her system; that familiar cold burn spreading fast, her body locked out of MethLumina's pull. Lori did herself next. She tossed the empty injectors into the trash as if they'd offended her.

"You know, it's wild what we can fix and what we can't," Lori said, shaking her head as she closed up the closet. Her voice was light, as if she wasn't condemning the dirty deals that made all those cures and poisons possible. Pharmaceutical companies played both sides: hooking you with one hand and selling your salvation with the other.

"Grab your gun," Lori said. "Whoever did Thornfield, they're not scared to shoot, and you're too much of an ass to die on me. You sign my paycheck."

Marti chuckled, moving back to her desk and popping open a drawer. Her gun was right where it always was. She slid it into the holster at her hip, feeling the weight settle against her. It didn't solve much. It hadn't in years. But she loved firing right next to some asshole's ear.

The office door clicked shut behind them, a sound that grated like a bad decision already made. The air outside bit at their faces, sharp and bitter, the neon glow of Falls City casting everything in garish, unflattering hues. The electric hum of the streets buzzed underfoot, alive, restless, as if the city itself was watching and judging.

"Stick to the plan," Marti muttered. Her gun pressed against her hip, heavy, reliable: the only promise that didn't feel like a lie.

"Since when do I not stick to the plan?" Lori shot back, pulling her jacket tighter.

Marti shot her a sidelong glance. "Do you seriously want me to list examples?"

"Don't confuse your failure to stick to plans," Lori said, "with mine."

Marti lit up a cigarette, exhaling smoke into the chill. "Yeah, whatever." She said it like a dare.

Chapter 11

The Handsome Dove didn't flaunt its reputation; it didn't need to. Hidden between a grubby pawn shop and a shuttered noodle stand, it waited, unassuming, like a predator confident in its camouflage. It sat on the northern border in Ironwood. One of the most accurate names of any of the districts in Falls City. A holographic hourglass shimmered above the doorway, faint enough to ignore unless you were looking for it.

"So this is supposed to be classy now?" Marti asked, flicking ash from her cigarette.

Lori shrugged. "It's trendy: retrofuturism or some bullshit. All style, no soul."

Marti smirked. "Sounds familiar." She crushed the cigarette underfoot and pushed the door open, stepping into what looked like someone's fever dream of an old cyber-punk utopia.

Inside, the air was thick with digital opiates and willing zombies. Holographic patterns crawled across the walls, shifting, twisting, dancing to an invisible rhythm. The lights pulsed in time with a low, vibrating beat that lodged itself in their chest cavities. Recliners lined the room, sleek and gleaming. People drooled in them, jacked into neural interfaces as if they'd already given up on reality.

At the center of it all was Dove. Cloaked in something that straddled tradition and tech without committing to either, he leaned against the glowing bar like he owned the place. Because he did. His sharp eyes scanned the room, not missing a thing.

"This guy just oozes subtlety," Lori whispered, earning another crooked grin from Marti.

"Looks more like he oozes bad cologne," Marti replied, her voice low.

The bar's LED countertop flickered as servers moved like shadows, slipping vials of MethLumina to their clients. Each transaction was nearly invisible, built into the rhythm of the place.

Lori stared at one of the hollow-eyed patrons in a recliner, their head lolled back, a satisfied, faraway smile on their face. "It's like the future from one of those ancient sci-fi movies," she muttered.

"Yeah, except with fewer laser battles and more mind-fucking drugs," Marti replied, scanning the room.

"This is supposed to be Garrison's hideout," Lori said, keeping her voice just above a whisper. "You think he's functional on this shit?"

"Microdosing, maybe," Marti said, her gaze lingering on a server tapping out a nervous rhythm on their tray as if it were something they couldn't stop. "Plenty of addicts keep it together just enough to screw everyone else over. And he's got lackeys for the dirty work."

"Sounds familiar," Lori said under her breath, her eyes cutting toward Marti.

But Marti didn't rise to the bait. She kept her focus on Dove, on the pulsing bar, on everything but the way Lori's hips swung when she walked.

Whatever this place was: a den, a haven, a sanctuary for the lost. It had its own rules, its own gravity, pulling people into their own little worlds. It reeked of desperation disguised as transcendence, and Marti hated it.

"We don't know what Garrison's planning," Lori said, her voice almost drowned out by the low hum of the room. "Or who he's got watching us."

Marti nodded, leaning in close enough for her words to stay private. "That's why we don't fuck this up."

"Always so reassuring," Lori deadpanned.

"Yeah, well, you're the one who came up with this bright idea," Marti said, her smile sharp enough to cut.

They moved further into the room, the door clicking shut behind them as if sealing them in. No turning back now.

"Two," Marti said, holding up her fingers and waving her payment card at Dove. Without a word, he brought over two doses of MethLumina. She stared at the shimmering capsules in her palm, their glow mocking her like little beacons of blissful absence. A million-to-one chance the NeuroLock would fail. With her luck, it might as well be a sure thing.

"You're hesitating," Dove said, his tone dripping with judgment reserved for those who've seen too much. The weight on Marti's chest twisted tighter, a lead blanket dipped in regret. She popped the capsule in her mouth, chased it with a swig of whiskey, and nodded to Lori, sliding her the other. Together, they swallowed like schoolkids trying to impress the babysitter.

Dove leaned in, his sharp gaze cutting through the haze of cheap whiskey and tension. "Open," he ordered, like a hall monitor. Both women opened wide, revealing empty mouths as Dove inspected them like smugglers at a border checkpoint. Satisfied, he handed them glasses of something and gestured toward the booths with a sardonic flick of his fingers. "Go. Enjoy your high."

Marti's eyes swept across the room, dancing over shrouded faces and clouds of cigarette smoke. Always pick a seat where you can see the entrance: rule number one. She moved through the murk, Lori trailing close behind, a shadow as she slid into a corner booth.

"You sure he'll show?" Lori's voice was a whisper, her nails picking at an old scar on the edge of the table. "What if today's the day he doesn't?"

Marti didn't blink. "Addicts don't take days off."

Lori's shoulders stiffened, but her eyes stayed darting, restless. "I just…" She paused, teeth sinking into her bottom lip. "What if the NeuroLock fails? I don't want"

"Focus," Marti interrupted, cutting her off. "Mission first. Nothing else matters."

The silence between them pressed heavy, thick with unspoken words that neither had the guts to say. Lori's hand rested inches from Marti's on the splintered wood of the table, close enough to touch but worlds apart. The door swung open with a creak so loud it might as well have been a gunshot.

Only Dove, Marti and Lori were conscious enough to watch as people came and never went.

"Eyes on me," Marti muttered. Lori didn't need telling twice. She locked onto Marti as if gravity itself demanded it, her green eyes swimming with all the things she'd been too afraid to admit. Marti didn't return her gaze; one problem at a time. And Lori? Lori was half the problem she couldn't deal with on her best day.

Marti sprawled back in the booth like she had all the time in the world. Across from her, Lori sat rigid, spine straight, hands folded tight. Every time the door groaned open, she flinched as if it was a gun being cocked.

Then, Garrison.

Jittery confidence wrapped up in a too-expensive suit, trying to pretend he wasn't clocking every pair of eyes on him. There weren't any. No one can see through eyelids.

The exchange at the counter was quick: credits transferred, MethLumina swallowed dry as if he didn't even need to taste it anymore. He rolled his shoulders once, then turned, scanning the room with that particular kind of detachment that men like him thought passed for control.

His gaze landed on them. His expression flickered, irritation settling over his face like an old habit. But he came over anyway.

"Hello, lesbians," he greeted as he slid into the booth across from them, voice thin and tight around the edges, already curling under the weight of the drug sinking into his system.

"Hello, cocksucker," Marti drawled, tipping her glass toward him as if this shithole den was some high-class cocktail lounge instead of a graveyard for reality. "Been a while."

He let out a breath that wasn't quite a sigh, wasn't quite anything at all except forced patience. "Why am I not surprised to see you here."

Marti smirked. "Funny how life's a bastard that way." She sipped her drink as if it wasn't watered-down piss and let her gaze drag over him with enough weight to be insulting. "You keeping busy?"

Garrison ran his tongue along the inside of his cheek before answering. "Enough." His eyes flicked to Lori: curious, maybe calculating. She only gave him a polite smile and stayed quiet. Smart girl.

"That's good," Marti murmured, leaning in enough to make him follow, closing that small space between them on reflex alone. Then she dropped it: "I've been watching porn." She let it hang there long enough for Garrison's brain to stutter before she added, "And by 'porn,' I mean amateur shit. Hidden camera stuff."

Garrison stiffened, just a fraction, but Marti caught it. He forced himself back against the seat as if he hadn't reacted at all. "Any good?"

She nodded, dragging her fingers along the rim of her glass as if she had nowhere better to be. "Yeah," she mused. "Came across something interesting: Marcus Thornfield." She tilted her head, watching for any tells as she said it. "You've heard of him." Not a question. Just fact. "Course you have; man's dead now." She let that settle between them before continuing, her smirk never slipping. "Anyway, turns out he was front and center in those little home-made tapes."

Lori shifted beside her, small movement but noticeable, but she didn't interrupt. This was Marti's game; she'd play it however she wanted.

Garrison didn't move except for one finger tapping out an erratic rhythm against his thigh beneath the table: tick tick tick. As if trying to recalibrate himself in real-time. Then he cleared his throat as if it might dislodge whatever lump had formed there when she'd said Thornfield.

"Oh yeah," Marti said, stretching the words like they were old leather, well-worn and smug with use. "Him and a few guys. Not all together: different nights, different setups. Real enthusiastic. Crystal clear for amateur spy porn." She shook her head, mock admiration smeared across her face before flicking her gaze toward Lori, con-spiratorial. "I swear there's hours of footage on those slip drives; I haven't even gotten through it all yet."

Lori snorted. "You like watching it in slow motion."

"True," Marti dragged it out, savoring each syllable like a slow sip of whiskey. "Makes you wonder if it caught what happened when Thornfield ate a bullet." She gave a lazy shrug and shot Garrison a grin sharp enough to cut glass. "You know? Did he film his own suicide? He filmed everything else."

A muscle in Garrison's jaw twitched as he swallowed down whatever instinct told him to run. He forced out a laugh: dry, brittle, useless. "Doubt it."

Marti hummed like she wasn't convinced, then tilted her head back toward Lori, amusement flickering behind her hooded eyes. "And can you believe it wasn't even the cops who found those slip drives?" She tsked and tapped two fingers against her temple in a mock salute before lifting her drink again. Watching Garrison's skin go too tight for his bones was almost as good as the liquor sliding down her throat.

He wiped his mouth once. Clasped his hands together tight where they sat on the table, as if they might betray him otherwise. Silence stretched thin between them like taut wire ready to snap. Then finally:

"You see anyone you know?"

Marti let out a breath before shaking her head, feigning exhaustion as if this little tête-à-tête was draining the life right out of her, as if she hadn't orchestrated the whole goddamn thing from the moment she sat down.

"Not yet," she admitted before flashing him another wicked grin and settling back into the booth. "But I needed a break from that endless ass pounding; I'll get back to it in the morning."

"Yeah, morning is in two hours, think you can wait?" Lori laughed.

Garrison flinched, just a fraction, but Marti caught it anyway, and it tasted sweet on her tongue.

She tipped her glass toward him one last time and smiled. "Nope, probably not."

Then Garrison blinked, the MethLumina dragging him under, shutting off the lights behind his eyes one by one. "The morning..." His lips twisted around the words as if they were math he couldn't quite work out anymore.

Marti shrugged. "Just kind of good at picking up on things." She paused. "So you know who's on the video?"

He slouched back into the booth, worn pleather groaning beneath his weight as he let out something that might've started as a laugh but curdled halfway through: low, bitter, gone before it ever touched his eyes.

"Thornfeeee…" The vowels stretched long and syrupy over his tongue.

For half a second, Garrison almost spoke, almost got something real past his teeth, but then the veneer cracked. His head wobbled forward once, twice. Then it lolled as if his strings had been cut. "Sssss… Thorf…" His jaw moved while the rest of him sagged into dead weight against the vinyl seat. "D… eyeeee…"

And then nothing; his whole body went limp, sinking deep into whatever void he'd been circling this whole time.

"Fuck," Marti hissed, fingers curling white-knuckled around the edge of the table as something hot and sharp stabbed through her ribs. The asshole went out before he said anything useful.

Lori's voice slipped in from somewhere beside her, soft, hesitant as if she already knew better than to ask but couldn't stop herself anyway:

"Was that a confession? Like… did he say 'die'? Or was he…"

Marti shot her a look so sharp it could've sliced bone clean through flesh. "Out," she snapped before some lackey clocked what had just happened and decided to make their night worse.

Lori hesitated for half a second but then did what she was told because she was smart when it counted most.

They slid out of the booth without another word, slid past Dove and hit the door slowly. No need to look rushed when every nerve screamed for speed.

Out on the street, Marti lit another cigarette and took a drag so deep it burned through whatever shock still clung to her ribs: all smoke and fire smothering thought beneath heat and nicotine.

Garrison gave nothing, not even an acknowledgement he knew about the tapes.

Didn't matter.

This wasn't going to end clean.

Chapter 12

The night had teeth. Cold bit into Marti's cheeks as she stood on the cracked pavement, arms crossed, a cigarette burning to the filter between her fingers. The holographic hourglass above the den flickered and stuttered, casting a sickly glow over the wet concrete. Lori shifted beside her, a stick of stim gum working between her molars. Neither of them said a word.

Lori was waiting for Marti to decide what to do. So was Marti.

Waiting felt like a gamble, and Marti wasn't winning much these days.

The sound of footsteps made her turn. Garrison stumbled out of the shadows as if he wasn't supposed to be there.

Marti's cigarette hit the ground and sizzled out in a puddle. "How the fuck?"

"Dove pulled me out of the goddamn MethLumina," Garrison said, shoving his hands in his coat pockets like a guilty teenager caught shoplifting. "Told me you two were screwing with him, said you tricked me too. Said I gotta fix it. So I did." His wrist flicked: tap, tap, tap, nervous energy leaking into the tic he couldn't control.

Marti snorted, blowing smoke she didn't have. "Look, Garrison," she said, her tone all glass and razors, "we know you were screwing Thornfield. It's on video. Maybe something shifted. Maybe he wanted more than you could give, started blackmailing you. You said it yourself: he was an evil bastard who needed to die."

"Did I say that?" Garrison's eyes darted skyward, desperate for some invisible lifeline, while his mouth kept running. "I didn't kill Marcus," he said, his voice trembling like a faltering lightbulb. "Yeah, he was blackmailing me, okay? But I had the situation handled. I wouldn't. I couldn't murder him."

Marti smirked, tilting her head as if she'd just heard the funniest joke of her life. "Garrison. Do you honestly expect me to buy that? You've got your greasy little fingers in every dirty deal Falls City's ever seen, but now you want us to believe you draw the line at murder?"

Garrison stiffened, crimson rising in his cheeks like a thermometer about to bust. "Of course," he spat. "I'm not a saint. But I didn't kill him."

Lori broke in, her voice sharp. "Then who did, huh? Someone put a bullet in him, and if it wasn't you, then who?"

Garrison's mouth twisted; that politician-ulcer grimace. His hands worked deeper into his coat pockets. "Why do you think I'm the only one he had dirt on? You said there were a lot of men in the videos."

Marti cursed not so silently, frustrate at how slick Garrison spoke, even when half stoned. Their videos would be useless without someting stronger.

"You two've been plowing through everyone in Falls City like it's your goddamn mission from God, dragging all our shit up into the light. I've got people calling me at city hall, whining about what you're doing. Like I'm supposed to fix it. Me!" He barked a humorless laugh. "You want a killer? Start just about anywhere else."

"Cut the bullshit!" Marti's voice cracked the night like a match striking dry wood. Her chest felt like it might explode. The Neurolock wrapped its clarity around Marti's skull and she hated it. "Just admit it, Garrison; stop wasting our time!"

"Fuck you," he snapped, eyes blazing. But then something shifted. The tic in his wrist wasn't just anxious fidgeting anymore. Tap, tap, tap. Frantic. Desperate.

Marti's gaze landed on his wrist. That wasn't a watch.

Her stomach hit the floor. "Oh, fuck me."

The moment shattered with screeching tires and heavy footsteps slamming into the silence. Garrison's face went whiter than his campaign posters.

"They're not mine!" he choked out, his voice climbing in pitch. He smacked his wrist as if it would summon his help.

The night turned predatory. Shadows detached themselves from walls, faces hiding under glossy black masks. Five, maybe six of them, moving like wolves closing in on a cornered deer.

"Hey assholes." The tallest one's voice carried over the wrecked street, icy and slow. He stepped forward, dragging a gloved hand along the edge of a knife. "You've been sniffing around places you shouldn't, lady."

"You fuck! You set us up!" Marti said as she stepped forward too close and ate a fist. She exhaled, wishing for another cigarette as she stepped back.

"Who the fuck are you guys?" Marti snapped, wiping blood from her lip with the back of her hand. Did Garrison have the connections? Stirling wouldn't pull this shit; why fuck with his own PI? Gardner? That bastard would wait until after she found his kid to come after her. Delacroix maybe? Or someone else on Thornfield's tapes? There were too many goddamn options, and she wasn't in the mood.

"Let me handle this." Garrison stepped forward, raising his hands, but somehow he'd drifted toward the cover of that overturned delivery truck. Smart positioning for a scared accountant. "I can make this right. Marti, just stay where you are."

"Back off now, Brucey," one of the men spat, his grin flashing yellow in the dim streetlight. "You know better than that."

Marti rolled her eyes. "Fucking ominous. Does everything have to be a dark monologue with you people?"

She noticed Garrison checking his phone's screen. Tap tap tap.

Really? Now? Her hand twitched toward her gun.

"Look," Garrison called out, his voice strangely steady for someone supposedly terrified, "just take what you came for. I kept my word."

The night exploded.

Gunshots: instant, deafening, sharp enough to drown out everything else. Marti didn't think; she grabbed Lori by the front of her jacket and yanked, dragging her down behind the nearest car. Gravel bit into her knees as they hit the ground hard.

From behind the truck's solid steel, she heard a voice, unnaturally calm: "Make it clean."

Who the fuck just said that?

"Shit," Lori muttered, flattening against the pavement, as if the asphalt held the secrets of invincibility.

"Not like that," Marti hissed. She hauled Lori upright by her collar. "Never lie flat in a gunfight. Knees, elbows. Move when I tell you."

Lori swayed, eyes wide and stunned, but she obeyed. For now. Small miracles. Marti wiped another streak of blood off her face with shaking fingers, muttering, "Christ, I need a hit."

Her face peeked above the car's hood for a second: long enough to see them. Two men. Where were the others? Dark clothes. One stocky, one lanky. They were still firing, their aim as sharp as kindergarteners drawing outside the lines. She pulled her gun and fired back, the sound punching through her ears, sharp and final.

"Stay quiet," she muttered at Lori, not sure she heard her. Not sure it mattered. The woman's breathing was ragged, panicked, but Marti didn't have time to soothe anyone. Didn't have time to calm herself. Every second stretched out, as if in a bad parody of an action movie. Guns. Yells. The stink of hot asphalt and sweat.

"Listen," Marti called across the alley, her voice dry and hoarse but loud enough. "You don't have to do this."

One of them stopped firing, stepped out of the shadows. His face was hard to make out, but his laugh carried: wet, guttural. "Lady, that's cute. But I think your clock's run out."

Before she could curse, more shots ripped through the air. The first one hit like an explosion in her ribs. Marti bit back a scream, though the pain radiated sharp, hot, feral. Survival instinct kept her on her knees. One arm still aiming; the other clutching the wound.

Lori's eyes, wide and shining, locked onto hers, and Marti could barely breathe under that look. "I'm fine," she lied through clenched teeth. Blood seeped between her fingers. Not much. Not yet. But enough to make her head swim.

Familiar territory.

She fumbled, grounding herself against the corner of the car. The men moved closer now, boots scraping on concrete. Marti took another breath, trying to steady her grip.

"Okay," she muttered to herself. "One for you, one for me." Another ragged breath. "Then we're fucking running."

Whether Lori heard didn't matter much.

The sound of two shots rang out.

"Run," Marti hissed, as if the whisper could cut through the air and slap Lori in the face. It didn't. Lori just blinked at her. Of course.

"Wh-" she started, but Marti didn't let her finish.

"Trust me," Marti snapped, her voice steadier than her hands, which curled into fists. The look she gave Lori could've stopped a bullet. Almost. "Go!"

Then the bullets started anyway.

The pavement exploded in front of them. Chunks of concrete spit up as the air filled with cracks and bangs louder than any thunderstorm Marti had been stupid enough to get caught in. She grabbed Lori by the arm and dragged, sprinting before her brain could convince her legs otherwise.

"Fucking run!" she barked again, breath burning in her throat. Her lungs felt like fire. Her ribs weren't doing great either. Perfect.

Lori stumbled beside her, trying to keep up but making noise that suggested she was a half-second from apologizing for existing. "I can't," she choked out, her voice between panic and determination, as if that would help.

Marti didn't slow down. "Run or die!" she shot back, though the words felt heavier leaving her mouth than they should've. The main street was up ahead, tantalizingly close, as if it could solve all their problems if they could just get there. But the darkness behind them wasn't playing fair. It had gotten bigger. Closer. Hungrier.

A sharp tug on her gut told her something was wrong, even before her eyes caught up with the shadowy figure that moved in ways people weren't supposed to. No time to think about it. No time to curse properly, or anything else.

"Go!" she yelled, shoving Lori ahead, as if that single act might erase the tight coil of dread sinking into her chest like an anchor.

But it wasn't enough. It never was.

Something heavy slammed into the back of her head: a baseball bat, maybe, or a fucking brick. Whatever it was, it hit hard enough to send a shockwave of pain through her skull. White-hot. Then black.

Her knees buckled. The alley spun, then tilted, as if someone had ripped the ground right out from under her.

"Marti!" Lori's voice was out there somewhere, frantic and too far away, and Marti hated how sad it sounded.

Hated that she could hear Lori's panic louder than the pounding in her own head.

But her mouth didn't work anymore. Neither did anything else. The shadows surged forward, swallowing everything whole.

And Marti let them.

Chapter 13

Marti came to with a groan; her head was splitting as if some twisted symphony was tuning up just to piss her off. A carousel of fractured light and shadow spun behind her eyes, and for a few nauseating seconds, she thought she might vomit all over herself.

Great. Dying or covering yourself with puke and then dying: what a menu of options.

The room swam into focus. It wasn't much to look at: four walls, dark and close, pressing in like an interrogation in some cheesy cop drama. She tried to shift, but the sharp pull on her wrists told her she was tied up.

And not in the fun way.

Perfect. Another goddamn Tuesday.

"Finally awake." The voice came from a corner cloaked in shadow, oozing through the air like oil slick on water. Cold, slimy, and condescending. "Thought you might be out for good."

"Yeah, well." Marti forced herself to sit straighter; the pain in her ribs flared up as her reward. She ground her teeth against the groan trying to climb out of her throat. "Sorry to disappoint."

She couldn't see him yet, but she didn't need to. She knew the type. Always lurking, always gloating. Always spilling their saliva and their egos into the same space. Frustration flared in her gut. "Where am I, asshole?"

"Touchy," the voice observes, a slow chuckle slithering out to underline it. "I wouldn't be so quick to bark questions. You're not exactly in a position to ask questions."

"No shit," Marti muttered. Every nerve in her body screamed, protesting the position of being baited or angry.

"Who the hell are you, and what the fuck do you want?" Marti snapped, trying to keep her voice steady; the duct tape and the throbbing headache weren't doing her any favors. She couldn't even see straight.

The guy smirked, the kind of smirk that said he'd watched too many bad gangster movies and thought he'd use to look cool.

Didn't work.

"You'll get your answers when I feel like it. Right now, you've got some explaining to do." His voice wasn't deep enough to match the tough-guy vibe. Amateur hour.

Marti tilted her head, squinting as if she could place his face through the haze of pain and whatever cheap after-shave he'd marinated in. "You look familiar. Why is that?"

He took a step closer, invading her space, his breath hot and sour. She grimaced. "No."

"Ah, fuck," Marti said, but her lips tugged into a smirk. "Henry Gardner, right? Daddy wants me to find you, and by want, I mean he would have killed me if I hadn't. Took me a second to place it under all the wannabe thug."

His face twisted, darkened; it was amazing how quickly some men unraveled the second they realized a woman knew more than they wanted her to. "Don't talk about my family," he growled.

Her lip curled as if she had a comeback loaded, but he cut it off with the flat of his palm: hard, fast, final. The crack of skin on skin echoed in the dead space between them. Her head snapped sideways, hair spilling like ink across her cheek. For half a second, everything held still. Just the hum of pain and the ghost of his touch burning red on her face.

Marti let out a low chuckle, toying with the danger in front of her. "Don't want me bringing up the nice folks who paid me to track your sorry ass down? Why am I here, then?"

No answer. Just a fist.

Her head wrenched to the side. A sharp burst of pain ignited along her temple. The room tilted, white-hot clarity cutting through the haze. She'd taken hits before, plenty, but sobriety had a way of making every nerve feel raw, every impact sharper than it used to be.

Fuck sobriety.

A slow drip of blood trailed down her throat. She ran her tongue over her split lip, tasting iron. What happened after that punch? Where had the time gone? Had she passed out? She flexed against the tape binding her wrists. Tighter than before. Awesome. "Touchy subject?" she said, her voice dry, hoarse. "Noted."

"I said," Henry spat, leaning in close again as if he was about to deliver something profound, "don't talk about my family."

Marti resisted the urge to roll her eyes. "Relax. No offense. Just laying out the situation here."

"The situation is," he shot back, dragging a metal chair closer across the floor, the legs screeching like a banshee, "you're here because I got paid to kill you. That's it. No other reason. Got it?"

Marti coughed hard to cover her gasp. Paid to kill her? But just not yet?

Goddammfuckshit. This was a bad place for a woman to be.

But Lori wasn't here. Henry hadn't caught her. Maybe. A knot tightened in her stomach. Lori. Please still be safe.

Marti leaned back, her chair creaking under her weight. Her odds weren't brilliant, but she'd had worse, probably. "Think I could bum a smoke?"

Henry snorted. "No. It's a disgusting habit."

"Says the guy who is going to commit murder. Perspective much? Or is my cigarette addiction somehow worse than your contribution to the graveyard?" She raised an eyebrow, mostly for her own amusement.

Fast as a whip crack, he jabbed a finger into her ribs. The pain fired sharp enough to make her gasp.

"Oh, is this where I'm supposed to learn a valuable lesson about my 'bad habits'?" she shot back, half-wheezing. "Because it sucks as a teaching moment. Try harder."

"That's just it," Henry said, dropping onto his chair with a thud. "You don't know shit. Not about me. Not about my family. Nothing."

Marti clocked Henry's hands. She'd seen those kinds of burns on people making Shadow. If they were sloppy beginners.

She straightened, her fingers testing the tape again behind her back. Still solid. "Funny," Marti said. "Your family seemed nice. Polite. Paid me upfront. Haven't killed me yet."

"Not yet," Henry barked a laugh, grating and joyless. "You're a crappy detective if that's your take. My dad? He's an asshole. You think he was nice to me? He had me running contraband before most kids were learning their ABCs."

Marti shrugged against her restraints. "I don't know, Henry," she said. "When I met him"—total lie; Lori handled the whole client schmooze in her stead—"he didn't seem half bad. Seemed like a guy who wanted his kid safe. Maybe I misread."

"You think he gives two shits about me? He doesn't." Henry leaned back, his chair rocking on two legs. "He wants his property back, that's all. I walked out the door with every recipe PharmaGardner hypes on the street. Took 'em straight to Devall Industries: my dad's precious competitor. You think I'm afraid of him?"

Marti blinked at him, unimpressed. "Devall hired you to kill me? Rich people are weird."

Henry sneered. "Not Devall. You're not exactly Sherlock Holmes with those keen observations, are you? You think he gives a shit about some little PI sniffing around?

News flash, asshole: you're just another pawn in this bull-shit game."

Marti laughed. "Well, daddy's paying me. Damn good money, too. So at least I'm getting something out of his bullshit game." She leaned as much as her restraints al-lowed. "How much do you get, Henry? For killing some washed up junkie?"

Henry smirked, but his eyes stayed dark. "My guy is paying a hell of a lot more than you'll ever understand."

Marti let the name hang words hang there for a split second. Most people would've backed off. Marti didn't play most people.

"Got a smoke? Last request and all," Marti said, as though they were discussing the weather. She hated to ask twice, but she wanted a cigarette.

Henry grinned, all teeth and venom. "Oh, I'm not going to kill you. You're going to kill yourself: tragic suicide. Very theatrical. Very... Thornfield."

Marti raised an eyebrow. "Suicide? What a twist. That shit's spreading faster than the flu."

Henry laughed, sharp and ugly. "The Thornfield Flu! That's what you caught!"

Now why did he bring up Thornfield?

Marti managed a tight smile. He was eating it up. Maybe she'd get that cigarette after all.

She coughed, rasping, and Henry waved her off like she was a buzzing fly. "Hey! Don't spread your germs on me."

"No worries, Henry," Marti said. "The Thornfield virus isn't contagious. You'd have to get close for that."

Henry puffed up with faux bravado. "Nah. I'm helping spread it. And when it's your turn, you'll die right on schedule. Convenient, huh?"

"Sure," she said with a shrug. "But if you really want this to sell, you'll need to let me have a cigarette. And a hit of Shadow. If my secretary hears from the M.E. that I'm clean, even for a second, she'll think something's up."

Henry tilted his head, squinting as if all the activity in his skull was crushing his single brain cell. "Huh. Yeah... That's true. Lemme check with the client."

Client? Shithead.

"Great, you do that. But seriously, I need a smoke first," Marti pressed, sharp but casual. Keep him talking. Keep him from noticing her pulse pounding in her chest.

Henry leaned in, sneering. "You know, this is what I mean. My dad hires losers. You're trash."

Marti smirked, but it didn't reach her eyes. "Can't argue there, Henry. We are who we are." She had to keep him distracted, but now her mind was racing toward a realization she didn't want to face.

Of course. It was all so obvious now. She'd been played.

Henry stood suddenly, snapping her back to the shitty reality of the moment. He pulled something out of his pocket: a knife. He flicked the blade open. He slashed it across the duct tape binding her to the chair.

"Don't even think about it," Henry sneered, eyes cold.

Marti watched him. Fucking idiot. Watched his hand dip into her coat pocket, fumbling for a lighter, then cigarettes. That's when she saw it. His eyes flicked down when he touched her gun.

Perfect.

She twisted hard, just as he pulled the gun from her pocket. The shot exploded in the small room, but the angle was off. Her movement had knocked his aim high. Plaster rained from the ceiling. No impact. No pain. He'd missed. Inches apart and the idiot missed.

Maybe.

He swung at her in frustration, but she was moving, lunging. They crashed sideways; the chair went with them in a splintering mess of shattered wood and scraped concrete.

Marti's hand closed on something solid: a thick chunk of broken chair leg. She swung upward. The wood connected with Henry's crotch. He let out a choked scream and buckled forward, trying to protect himself.

The gun hit the floor and skittered out of reach.

Good enough.

Marti didn't waste time scrambling for it. Momentum first; weapons later. She drove an elbow into his face, following with a knee to his ribs. Fast, vicious attacks to keep him off balance.

Henry was twice her size and all brute strength, swinging with raw force but no precision, like a meathead brawler who thought power solved everything. It didn't. Not when she knew how to move.

Another wild punch flew past her.

Not sloppy.

Pain detonated in her chest as one of his fists connected: a solid hit that sent her reeling back, blurring her vision.

Her lungs seized as if she'd been kicked by a horse.

Throat, eyes, groin, knees: the holy quartet of pain, the weak spots that turned mountains into rubble. Some old academy instructor had drilled that into her head years ago. You're not here to fight fair; you're here to win.

"You fucking cunt," Henry spat through bloodied lips, wiping at his mouth as if he could erase the hits she'd landed.

"Good," Marti breathed.

She feinted left, then drove the jagged chair leg straight into his knee.

Henry howled and staggered as pain ripped through him, but he wasn't done swinging yet. Another fist came at her temple, slower but still dangerous. She ducked late, too late; his knuckles clipped just enough to send stars ripping across her vision.

Her ears rang.

Her body screamed at her to drop back, to breathe, but fuck that.

She planted her boot between his legs with ruthless efficiency, then went for the eyes like a feral cat that had finally had enough of someone's shit.

Henry screamed something unintelligible as Marti clawed at his face. Maybe a curse, maybe a prayer. It ended when she drove a fist straight into his throat.

His breath hitched in strangled agony as he stumbled backward.

She didn't wait for him to recover.

The broken chair leg smashed against his left knee once, twice, a third time to make sure he fucking remembered this moment forever.

Henry hit the concrete, struggling through shock and fury as he reached for anything to help pull himself up, but Marti was already moving.

As she turned to grab the gun across the floor, fingers barely brushing metal, something viselike clamped around her ankle and yanked.

"The fuck," she hissed as gravity betrayed her.

They collapsed together; his weight slammed into her like dead weight. Only for half a heartbeat before every muscle in her body snapped into action.

A scramble of limbs and force: Henry trying to pin her down; Marti twisting like something sharp in the dark.

Her leg hooked high around his neck before instinct could warn him what was coming.

Triangle choke locked tight. His grunt turned into a ragged choke as she wrenched down on his trapped arm, tendons stretching past their limit with precision.

He clawed at her ribs, desperate now. This wasn't some barfight anymore; this was someone who knew exactly how far bodies could bend before they broke and pushed past that point without hesitation.

"You feel that?" she growled through gritted teeth as she adjusted position. The perfect shift of leverage over resistance.

His struggles turned erratic.

That little pop.

The wet crack.

His scream.

It rattled inside her skull before trailing into something weaker: something small and ruined beneath adrenaline and pain.

Marti let go of him. No use holding dead weight when you already won.

Her knuckles were next. The soft spot beneath his ribcage became target practice beneath precision: liver shot after liver shot tearing through whatever fight he had left until desperation abandoned him.

Henry flailed one last time. One last swing at her face that barely connected.

He puked.

That was new.

"Not done yet," Marti exhaled, not quite laughing but not not laughing, as she pressed one last boot against his face with enough force to knock him back flat against the ground where he belonged.

His skull smacked concrete with a dull thud.

Silence.

Blessed fucking silence.

And just like that, it was over.

For now.

Marti fought to steady her breathing, the metallic taste of victory mingling with relief that while he'd tried to kill her, at least she wouldn't have to burn her clothes or scrub invasive hands from her skin.

With her heartbeat beating at an almost human rate, she slapped at his pockets, her fingers trembling. His wallet.

Proof of life for Kevin.

She was on her feet a second later, shoes slipping on the blood-slick floor. Snatched her gun and with one glance back at Henry: broken, bleeding, unconscious. She sprinted out of the room. Her pulse roared in her ears, her chest burning with every step. She didn't care. All she needed now was an exit. That, and maybe a hit.

"No rest for the wicked," she muttered, rounding the nearest corner. "Or the stupid."

Marti kicked through the warehouse doors, gulping air like it was free. Her knuckles were sticky with blood; Henry's or hers, who even knew anymore? The parking lot yawned open before her, rain drenching every shadowy corner, every puddle shimmering under the buzz of streetlights that barely lit the maze ahead.

"Right," she muttered to herself, sprinting into the downpour as if she wasn't bleeding from half her body. "Just keep moving, Marti. Solid plan."

The puddles sloshed under her boots, and her lungs screamed with every step. The city sprawled out like a sadistic board game: go one way, lose your head; go the other, find five more assholes like Henry waiting to finish the job they'd botched.

Was he even with the original gang?

A sharp corner loomed ahead, and Marti pushed toward it with the grace of a drunk raccoon: slipping, skidding, nearly face-planting before she caught herself.

She leaned against the damp wall for a second, rain streaming off her hair and into her eyes. A dark alley gaped across the street as if it wanted to eat her. Sounded sexy right now. "Alley it is," she said, limping toward it on legs she wasn't sure worked.

Once in its hands, the night closed in, thick and quiet but somehow louder than her thoughts. The shadows clawed down the walls as if they were alive, but Marti cared only about keeping her head attached to her neck. She collapsed against some broken crate, the wood biting into her back as she tried and failed to catch her breath. Her head throbbed where Henry had cracked her with... what was it, a pipe? A wrench? Didn't matter; it hurt like hell either way.

She winced, running shaky fingers through her hair, which came back wet: too much of it blood. "Fantastic." Her voice was no louder than a whisper. She rolled her wrist, testing the damage. Nope, broken. Great. Add that to the grand tally of reasons tonight sucked.

She slapped her body. Not a single inhaler in a single pocket. No Fentafill, no nothing. How could an addict have nothing?

Her stomach twisted before her brain caught up. Where was Lori? Marti squeezed her eyes shut and prayed to whatever deity might still hate her less than the others. Lori had been. No, was. Alive when this clusterfuck started.

Maybe she'd made it out.

She had to.

Lori was smart. Resourceful. Annoyingly clever. She'd probably already stocked the office fridge with blood bags and vodka for round two of fixing Marti's dumbass decisions. That thought brought a sharp, bitter chuckle that caught in her throat.

But the thought didn't stick. Something heavier slithered in right after, cold and coiled at the base of her skull.

How did they know?

Devall's hired goons: was he the client? They had been waiting for them. Waiting as if they'd read a script. Marti spat blood onto the ground and ran a trembling hand down her face.

Someone's been talking.

And only Lori knew.

The air in the alley stank: damp garbage mixed with something metallic that screamed "your own guts" if she wasn't careful. Marti squinted through the dark, making out the walls pressing in around her. Her vision blurred again, her brain scrambling to keep up with the thoughts running wild in her head.

She wanted to move. She had to move. Find Lori. Figure out who sold them out. It wasn't Lori. That was just stupid talking. Garrison knew. Everyone at the Handsome Dove knew they were there. Dove knew.

And what she knew now was...

Get out of this alley before someone decided she'd make a nice addition to the city's body count. But she sat there, bloodied, broken, and choking down the irony of it all.

"Not like this," she growled into the silence, voice raw. And then, quieter, to herself: "Please."

Chapter 14

The alley reeked of piss and dumpster rot, as if someone had bottled up the essence of this city and splashed it against the walls for fun. Marti leaned there, one hand pressed to her ribs as if trying to hold herself together. Blood dripped from her busted lip, cold against her chin. She spat the rest onto the asphalt, a dark smear in the dim light.

"Fantastic," she muttered, drawing in a breath that sent fire lancing up her side.

A shot to the ribs, three to the face, and a boot that had tried, and nearly succeeded, to crush her windpipe. She'd had worse. Probably. If her memory wasn't so hazy, maybe she could rank her pain.

"Focus," she hissed, squeezing her eyes shut to reset her balance. When she opened them again, she was back on her feet, the wall there to steady her. Her left hand held her ribs, her right held the wallet. Proof of life, a little.

"Where the fuck is my gun?" she gurgled, as if the rat in the dumpster could answer.

She'd taken it. Hadn't she? Dropped it? Probably.

The street stretched ahead of her, narrow and crooked; the kind of place tourists avoided and locals tried to forget. It pulsed with something slimy and alive, as if the city itself was breathing, watching, waiting. Shadows moved in the corners of her vision where nothing should have been moving.

"Move," she told herself. And she did. One step at a time.

Her footsteps echoed off the walls, too sharp, too loud, as if the city was mocking her attempt at stealth. Every sound, a distant hum, a scrape of metal, rattled her nerves like they were strung tight. And maybe they were. A sadistic knot.

She caught herself muttering under her breath, "You've got this. You can do this." The words sounded like a lie, but they were all she had.

It was getting weird. Seeing things weird. Hearing things weird. Probably the blood loss. Or the Shadow cravings.

Or both. Fuck if she knew. She tightened her grip on the wallet and kept moving, letting her instincts guide her: stay to the walls, stay in the shadows, keep your eyes open.

The backstreets wound on ahead like a bad dream, sloppy and aimless. Every corner felt like a trap waiting to spring. Every flicker of light felt like it had teeth. Marti's boots hit the pavement too hard, her body too bruised to attempt subtlety. She kept her head up. She didn't flinch. Weakness stunk worse than fear in this part of town, and there was already plenty of that.

"Almost there," she lied. Some part of her wasn't sure where there was anymore, but stopping was never an option.

She spotted Rat before he spotted her. He was basement-level shit. Rat leaned in a grimy doorway, hands shoved in his dirty coat, his belt sagging as if it was giving up on him entirely. He looked up when she stepped into his line of sight, his face crinkling in a way that almost, almost resembled concern.

"You look like you crawled out of an incinerator," Rat said, his voice matching the alley's general ambiance.

Marti ignored the jab, ignoring everything except the inhaler-shaped bulge in his pocket. "Shadow?" Her voice was low, tight, desperate enough to cut through her usual bullshit.

Rat eyed her, slow and deliberate, as if he was cataloging her injuries just in case she keeled over mid-deal. "You look like shit, Marti," he said. "How much you need?"

"I need enough to keep moving," she snapped. And then, quieter, "No cash. Will this cover it?" She held up the wallet, her fingers reluctant to let go of it even as she offered it up.

Rat took the cash out of it; twenty was enough for a pack of smokes. He gave it back. "Anything else?"

"You want my gratitude?"

Rat barked a laugh and shook his head. "Fuck no. That's worth jack shit without. But..." He trailed off, rubbing the back of his neck as if he was annoyed with himself, and pulled out the inhaler anyway. "You gave me some when I fucked you over at the Gung Ho. Call it even."

Marti snatched it out of his hand before he could change his mind. Her index finger brushed the trigger, a motion so familiar it was almost muscle memory. She raised it halfway to her lips when he leaned in and muttered, "Careful, huh? You look like someone's gunning for you."

Ah, fuck. She couldn't afford to get fucked up right now. Not until she was somewhere safer.

She glared at him through blood-crusted lashes. She hated the truth sometimes. Most times. "Gunning. Yeah," she said, sliding the inhaler into her jacket.

"Thanks for the hit," Marti sneered, voice slicing through the air like a shard of broken glass. She gripped the inhaler like a lifeline, her knuckles pale against the cheap black plastic. With a glance over her shoulder, sharp, paranoid, she leaned against the piss-soaked wall: the kind of wall you slid down and died against.

Addicts feel safest when they're high.

She didn't hesitate. Shadow hit her lungs in one deep pull, and the world shifted, flipped. Warmth flowed through her veins like hot honey, soothing the raw edges of her nerves. Pain dulled. Chaos clarified. For a single, fleeting moment, everything made sense. Then the moment passed, and reality crashed down.

Rat was gone. How many hits did she take? She was running on Shadow fumes.

"Alright, you pathetic bitch," she muttered to herself, shoving off the slimy brick wall she'd been leaning on. Her voice was low, nearly drowned out by the distant hum of neon. "Get moving. Magic's not gonna just fall in your lap."

Her boots slapped against wet pavement, each step pulling her closer to the office: her safe haven, her sanctuary, her fucking asylum. She didn't check the blood she knew was staining her shirt. It hurt. It always hurt. That was life. She'd be fine.

By the time she slammed through the door, it felt like every beat of her heart might be her last. Lori's head snapped up from her desk and took in the soaked woman standing before her.

"You look like shit," Lori said, rising as Marti stumbled into the chair opposite her desk.

"Thanks, sweetheart. You always know what to say."

Then she saw the blood. "Jesus Christ, Marti!" Lori was around the desk in an instant, her face draining of color. Her hands trembled as they hovered over Marti's wounds. "I've been calling you for hours. Hours! What happened to you?"

"I'm here, aren't I?" Marti batted Lori's hands away, though her shoulders sagged like a deflated tire. "Looks like you're still breathing."

"They stopped chasing me once I hit Raderson Road," Lori said, her voice cracking as she dropped to one knee beside the chair. She gripped the armrest until her knuckles went white. "Just stay here, let me get everything."

"Yeah, yeah, not going anyw. Fuck that hurts."

"Then don't do it," Lori said as she opened the closet. She turned when Marti groaned.

She froze.

"Why are you gushing blood in my office?" Lori stood, one hand clutching a battered med kit, the other pointing accusatory at the dark stain spreading across Marti's shirt.

Marti took a drag off her cigarette (when did she light that?), her smirk as unsteady as her hands. "Would've mentioned it, but you seemed busy trying to juggle that moral crisis. Relax, it's just a knuckle scratch. Ring, maybe."

"Maybe?" Lori's voice pitched higher, as if bordering on a full meltdown. "You're leaking like a bad faucet and cracking jokes? Jesus Christ, Marti."

Marti shrugged, winced, and gestured toward her shirt. "It's unfair how blood always makes everything dramatic. You want the fun part or the bad part first?"

"Neither." Lori slammed the med kit onto the cluttered desk, sending loose papers fluttering to the floor. "I want you to shut up so I can keep you from dying on my god-damn carpet."

"Fair." Marti leaned back in the chair and exhaled smoke toward the rain-streaked window. "Henry Gardner's alive. Or was, until about ten minutes ago. Or hours ago."

"Gardner?" Lori froze mid-rummage, her hand hover-ing over a roll of SynthoSkin. "The kid Kevin hired you to find; the supposed runaway?"

"Yeah, not so much a missing kid. Hired muscle. Bad at it, though." Marti flicked ash onto the floor. "Turns out, Daddy's boy switched teams. He's been playing errand boy for Devall: maybe since he left, maybe longer."

The cigarette trembled between her fingers, but she took another drag, the smoke slicing through the chemical tang of the office. Lori yanked out Synthoskin, ViaRevive and gloves, her movements jagged. "Why didn't you start with that instead of bleeding all over my desk?"

"Didn't think you'd appreciate the context." Marti snorted, her laugh bitter. "We scrapped in a warehouse, I think. He dragged me somewhere. Though the gentleman offered this lady a chair. He's worse off. But this isn't just about Henry anymore. Someone hired him. And I think Kevin Gardner's got his fingers somewhere deeper than I thought."

"Deeper how?" Lori's gloves snapped on with a sharp pop. She dropped to her knees and started peeling away Marti's jacket. Blood smeared her gloved hands. "Christ. Hold still, would you?"

Marti hissed when Lori tugged her shirt up. "A little higher and you owe me dinner."

"Oh, fuck off." Lori grabbed a tube of ViaRevive, squeezing the gel onto the wound with force. She ignored Marti's sharp inhale. "Is this a gunshot?"

"Uh, nnnooooo…"

Lori looked at Marti's shirt again, at the gunpowder. She gave Marti a stern glare. "Keep talking. Gardner's deeper where?"

"Everywhere, I think." Marti motioned with her hand, sending Lori scurrying to get the whiskey. Marti sipped as Lori worked.

"Start with Thornfield. He's dead. Suppose Kevin thought Henry joined Thornfield's crew. Father can't have son working for competition; instead of killing Henry, Kevin killed Thornfield, made it look like suicide. Figured Henry would get the message to come home."

"And?" Lori nodded, holding a Fentafill in her palm.

"Kevin got it wrong. Henry never went to Thornfield: he went to Devall. So that message wasn't received." Marti's voice was cool. She downed the pill with a sip.

"Now Kevin's taken out the wrong kingpin for nothing, and once he finds out where Henry really is…" Lori's face went pale as she slapped the SynthoSkin onto Marti's ribs.

"He'll move against Devall," Lori whispered. "And we're caught in the middle."

"The whole fucking city would be caught in the middle," Marti corrected.

"So we're supposed to, what? Turn Henry over to his father? Get him killed? Get Devall killed? Start a war?"

Lori stared at her, the words landing harder than the rain hammering against the cracked window. "What are you going to do?" she asked, breaking the silence.

Marti snorted, her smirk twisting into something genuine, if broken. "Figure out how to charm some snakes. Let me smoke in peace."

Lori didn't say a word, though the silence sat heavy. She cleaned up. Blood sought refuge in the cracks of the hardwood while Lori wiped up what she could.

"I've gotta tell Ari Stirling," Marti said, breaking the quiet. She lit a cigarette, took a drag that made her cough, then took another. "He's the client. He needs to know what I've figured out."

Cough.

"It's a theory, Marti," Lori snapped, turning to face her. "You don't go to a client with just a theory." She crossed the room, brushing ash off Marti's lap as if it was a goddamn reflex, then froze. "Oh, shit. Marti." Her voice broke as she undid the top buttons of Marti's shirt and saw the mottled bruises spreading across her chest. "Oh no."

Marti glanced down, shrugged, and gave a dry cough that tasted like stale whiskey. "Tell me the truth. I kind of rock the bruised-up look, don't I?"

"No. No, Marti, you fucking don't," Lori said, her fingers hovering over the wreckage as if her touch would make it worse.

Marti's nipples perked up in response, because of course they did. Traitors.

"Okay, not Ari. Yet. Set up a meeting with Kevin Gardner. Tomorrow morning," Marti said, brushing Lori's hands away and draining the last mouthful of whiskey from the bottle she'd been clinging to. She smeared the leftover taste across the back of her wrist. "Put that wallet somewhere safe. I need a shower."

"You need a hospital."

"I just had Nurse Lori give me her ministrations. Don't you trust your skills?"

"How do you even know that word? Towels are on the counter," Lori sighed, already moving. She grabbed the wallet and tossed it into her desk drawer; her irritation painted in broad, angry strokes.

Marti hesitated. That thing that sat between them: the unspoken bullshit caught in her throat. "Listen, kiddo."

Lori froze mid-spin, eyebrow cocked.

"...Forget I said that," Marti muttered. "Look, I'm going home for a shower. Sleep. Don't hang around here. It's not safe. Henry's still out there, and I don't know what the hell he's cooking up. Once we talk to Kevin." Her pointer finger jabbed the air as if a cigarette-pointer kind of pep talk might help. "I'll come up with a plan for him and Ari. Something that actually works."

Lori didn't respond, didn't say anything at all. Marti hated that. Silence was heavier when Lori wielded it.

Marti hauled herself up from the chair, nearly knocking Lori over in the process. "I'll see you in the morning," she said, walking toward the door.

"Marti."

"Nope," Marti cut her off without turning. She slammed the door behind her.

The night met her outside with the grit and stink of city leftovers. Marti dug out her phone, scrolled for a name, thumb hovering for a moment before she hit dial.

"Pauline, baby," she rasped when the line clicked open. "I need you. Get to my place. Now."

Chapter 15

Ignoring the way her ribs screamed in protest, Marti slid into her car. Small, black, discreet: just enough speed to outrun trouble but not enough shine to invite it. The electric engine purred as she rolled out into the sluggish crush of evening traffic.

The city flickered past in neon slashes and restless shadows. Cops wandered the streets as zombified as everyone else, at least until you hit the Blightwood neighborhood. Then everything just died. Ravencrook Street waited for her, lined with brick ghosts of a city that had stopped giving a shit decades ago.

She wedged into her usual spot between a rusted-out delivery van and a holographic parking meter stuttering on its last legs. Her apartment building loomed above: three stories of peeling paint, cracked windows streaked with the grime of a thousand midnight betrayals.

Marti sucked in a breath, braced, and dragged herself out of the car. Her side flared hot as she pressed a hand against her ribs, as if that might actually help anything. The stairs weren't stairs. They were a goddamn punishment.

Anything not to take the vertical moving coffin.

Metal groaned under each step; she gritted her teeth, gripping the railing tighter than she'd ever admit. By the time she hit the third floor, sweat slicked her skin and fire burned in her side.

The stairwell door creaked open to her dim hallway: scuffed linoleum, chipped walls, and the faint scent of old cigarettes that had seeped into everything years ago. She exhaled, steeling herself for the last few steps home.

And there she was. Waiting.

Pauline sat on the hallway floor as if she had all the time in the world, spinning a gold inhaler between her fingers. She grinned that sharp little grin that made Marti's stomach tighten in ways she'd rather not acknowledge.

Yes she would.

"You look like shit," Pauline said. "Lucky for you, I've got just what you need, baby." She twirled the inhaler once more before catching it mid-air like a magician finishing a trick. "I'll be gentle," she added with mock sincerity. "I promise."

Inside, the apartment was dark except for the warm pool of light from a single lamp in the corner. Marti dropped onto her battered couch with a grunt, fingers fumbling at the laces of her boots before giving up and yanking them off.

Wet squelch. Blood smeared inside one boot; both socks were soaked through. Perfect fucking ending to a perfect fucking night.

Pauline kneeled in front of her without invitation, hands warm against Marti's calf as she peeled away ruined socks like they were evidence at a crime scene.

She didn't even ask.

A sharp breath hissed between Pauline's teeth when she saw the crimson-streaked skin.

"You're a mess," Pauline murmured, voice soft but still edged with something gritty.

Marti let out something close to a laugh and let her head drop back against the couch cushions. "You should see the other guy," she muttered, though maybe not as cocky as usual because fuck, everything hurt right now.

Amazing how Shadow, whiskey and Fentafill were sometimes, sometimes not enough.

Pauline traced careful fingers along Marti's shin as if she was considering something dangerous.

Marti should stop this before it went anywhere. But then again, if she knew how to stop things before they spiraled out of control, she wouldn't be here in the first place.

"You're getting in the shower," Pauline said, already yanking Marti's blood-crusted shirt away from her skin. "I'm not touching that ass until you're clean."

Marti clenched her jaw as the fabric peeled away, sticking to half-healed wounds. Pauline worked fast, fingers steady, not gentle. The ruined shirt hit the floor with a slap.

She moved to the pants next. "This is gonna suck, baby," she warned, tugging at the waistband. "But don't worry; I got you." Her voice was warm, amused, as if this was funny to her.

The pants were worse than the shirt: stiff with dried blood and alley filth, clinging as if they had a grudge. Every pull sent fresh waves of pain through Marti's battered body, but she gritted her teeth and let Pauline work.

"Can I?" Pauline gestured at what was left: bra, underwear, scraps of fabric barely holding together anyway.

Marti gave something that might've been a shrug and leaned back against the couch cushions. Too tired to care if

Pauline stripped her bare and tossed her into traffic. Both would probably happen before sunrise anyway.

Pauline didn't wait for more than that. She worked quick, efficient, until Marti was raw and exposed in every way possible.

"Come on," Pauline said, gripping Marti's wrist and hauling her up as if she wasn't all bruises and open wounds. Surprising strength for someone whose biggest daily struggle was balancing a tea tray. "Shower."

Water roared through the pipes, steam curling up. Pauline adjusted the temperature without checking: that perfect line between almost-scalding and barely-merciful that burned grime off without cooking flesh.

Before Marti could step inside, Pauline shoved something into her lips: an inhaler, sleek metal cool against her fingers. "Half a hit."

Marti sucked in. Pauline yanked it back with a laugh before she got a proper inhale. "That's all you get! Now hurry up; your ass better be clean before I finish making coffee."

She was gone, vanishing through the doorway while Marti stood there blinking before stepping under the spray.

Heat hit first, then pain, then relief as blood and foul swirled down the drain in slow ribbons of red and brown and whatever else she'd picked up in the fight. She braced herself against the tile and breathed through it until enough dulled that she could function again.

By the time she dragged herself into the main room, towel barely clinging to one shoulder, Pauline was at the table with two cups of coffee steaming.

"You only own two mugs," Pauline observed as Marti dropped onto the bed and grabbed one without saying 'thanks'. "You ever think about getting more?"

Marti took a long swallow, too much too fast, let it sear all the way down before answering. "Only got two hands," she muttered once she could breathe again. "Only need two cups."

Pauline shook her head as if that logic belonged in some record book for dumbest arguments ever made, but still didn't push further. Which was exactly why Marti tolerated her more than most people who tried forcing their way into her life.

Liked her, even. As much as you could ever like a drug addict.

Marti stretched out on her bed after that, arms at her sides in a position that hurt least, and watched as Pauline rose from the chair and started stripping down in that nonchalant way of hers: pants first, always pants first. Then shirt next in one smooth motion that left bare skin glowing under low light as if some painting come to life from another century.

Marti reached out, fingers drifting along Pauline's jaw. The dim light caught on her skin, turning everything soft around the edges, except for the sharp pull just under Marti's ribs where desire and SynthoSkin tangled into something indecipherable.

"I've been thinking about this all day," Marti lied, voice rough, cutting through the silence between them.

Pauline smiled like she believed it, as if she wanted to believe it. "Me too." Another lie.

Junkies always lied. They always pretend otherwise.

The sheets twisted beneath them as Pauline shifted closer, catching Marti's mouth in something tentative at first, like poking a bruise to see if it still hurt. It did. Marti's hand found the curve of her lower back, fingers pressing into warm skin as she dragged her in deeper. The kiss turned sharp in half a second; less like a slow burn and more like drowning on dry land.

Pauline sighed against her, bodies slotting together as if they'd done this a thousand times before and would do it a thousand times again no matter how much sense it didn't make. No hesitation, no frantic rush; just that quiet hum of inevitability creeping under Marti's ribs.

She tasted like Shadow and coffee, and fuck if that wasn't exactly what Marti needed.

For half a breath, their foreheads brushed before Pauline kissed her again, hungrier now, fingers twisting into Marti's hair as if holding on might stop the ground from rushing up to meet them. Like either of them had ever been that lucky.

"You're about to have a great fucking night," Pauline murmured, setting the sleek gold inhaler on the bedside table like an offering at some altar of bad decisions. "Golden Shadow," she added when Marti didn't grab it. "Evelyn got me the good stuff."

Fucking fantastic. Another drug about to tear through the streets. The first half hit did nothing for Marti, though she was always willing to try a new drug. Twice.

Pauline climbed onto the mattress and over Marti with something sharp beneath all that teasing amusement curving at her lips.

"Golden Shadow doesn't hook you," she said softly. "It just... opens doors."

Marti frowned slightly, even as her mouth watered at the scent rising off Pauline's skin. The musk of sweat, sex, and something metallic beneath. "Doors to what?"

Pauline's fingers ghosted over Marti's bruises like she was tuning an instrument. "To each other," she said simply.

Her mouth curved against Marti's jaw when she dipped lower, breath warm where pulse points stuttered under careful hands, before whispering against parted lips:

"I promise, you're going to love this, baby."

Then she moved up the bed, deliberate as sin, one knee settling on either side of Marti's head, heat pressing down until there was nowhere else to go but here. "I want you front-row for this," she murmured, reaching for the inhaler. Pressed it up against Marti's lips as if sealing a deal with the devil himself. "Big breath in." A slow roll of her hips as she tilted her chin down, dark eyes locked onto hers. "And when you exhale, do it in me, baby."

Marti looked up, drinking in the view: the soft insides of Pauline's thighs, the neatly trimmed dark curls above her pussy, the curves of her ass just out of reach.

She took a pull from the inhaler, held it deep in her chest until it burned, pressed her lips against lips, then let it out in a steady stream.

This time, something changed.

Smoke unfurled from Marti's mouth. Not gray this time, but shimmering gold. It didn't drift up like before. It reached. Fingers of fog curled around Pauline's thighs deliberately, caressing her skin like they knew the way. And when Pauline shivered, Marti felt it mirrored in her own ribs.

A tug in her chest, electric and strange. Her breath caught. Not from arousal this time, but recognition.

A heartbeat that wasn't hers thudded in her temples.

Pauline took her hit next without hesitation. When their eyes met again, everything tilted sideways.

The room was still there, but not in one piece. The sheets rippled like ink on water. The shadows gained weight; light gained texture. They were still touching, but suddenly more than flesh pressed them together.

Something deeper threaded through them, some pulse beneath the sex-hot haze. A rhythm neither had made but both were following now.

They weren't two bodies anymore.

More like one experience observed from two angles.

Marti's vision wavered with every movement, colors shifting from deep purple to electric blue to blood-red and back again as Pauline worked herself open with every flick and thrust.

Her breath hitched; her body shuddered like something was uncoiling inside her. Faster now. Fingers driving deep before slipping free again, dragging wetness up over swollen flesh only to plunge back down. Out, up, around, down, in. Again and again until nothing about her seemed solid anymore.

Then came the sound: a low keening that built into something louder, rougher; a thunder rolling inside her chest before breaking free. The first spasm rocked through Pauline so hard that Marti felt it in her teeth. Then came another. And another. Until wet heat spilled down in waves across waiting lips and tongue and chin.

Marti swallowed hard, the taste of Pauline still slick on her mouth as she found words again, but didn't bother using them. She watched as the last tremors ran through Pauline's shaking body: aftershocks of pleasure pulsing beneath flushed skin like a dying star refusing to burn out.

Pauline's hands went still. She exhaled, then moved, deliberate, as she lifted a knee and swung it over Marti, breaking their connection. Marti let out a sound; half whimper, half curse, as Pauline's clit disappeared from view.

Pauline's fingers formed out of smoke for just a second before pressing into Marti's mouth.

Marti didn't hesitate. She sucked, licked, pulled, as if she could taste the whole damn universe if she tried hard enough. Her tongue traced every slick remnant of Pauline's pleasure as if the world was ending and this was the only thing keeping her alive.

Pauline laughed: a soft, breathy thing, as she pulled her fingers free and smoothed them over Marti's cheek, careless and smug.

But when the sound stretched, twisted. It wasn't just happening outside Marti's ears anymore. It echoed inside her skull like a feedback loop of pleasure unspooling into something vast and unknowable.

She blinked again, and for a moment, saw herself in Pauline's eyes. Not a reflection exactly, but an awareness: recognition folding in on itself.

She felt Pauline tremble, and knew exactly what the orgasm had felt like from the inside out.

Felt it pass through her own nerves like smoke through cloth.

And then—

Marti lurched upright, same as before, but this time as though yanked out of sync rather than waking up alone. Something tore and left behind an ache where connection used to be humming steady between them.

That sudden emptiness after being wrapped in someone else's mind made everything feel more silent than silence should be.

What had just happened?

Chapter 16

Marti woke up drowning.

Not in water; just sweat, soaking cold through the sheets, clinging to her ribs like a second fucking skin. She sucked in air too fast, too sharp, and choked on it. Her heartbeat was a fist slamming against the inside of her skull.

Pauline was still asleep beside her, breathing slow, peaceful, as if Marti hadn't just...as if last night hadn't...

"Fuck," she whispered, voice scraped raw.

The golden inhaler sat on the nightstand, gleaming in the early light. Taunting her. Shadow never hit like that before. Never cracked open the world and made it bleed. Never left her wondering if she'd clawed her way back from something that wasn't supposed to let go.

She shoved aside the twisted sheets and stood on legs that barely held her. The bathroom was ten steps away. It felt like a fucking pilgrimage.

Cold water, first thing: splashed across her face, down the back of her neck. She gripped the sink, breathing hard through parted lips, waiting for something to settle that wouldn't.

Her reflection stared back at her, washed-out and dead-eyed. Same old wreckage: exhaustion carved into cheekbones too sharp, lips pulled tight over teeth she half-expected not to be hers anymore.

She fucking hated this part: the collapse after the bad high, when everything came rushing back as if it had been waiting for her to sober up before tearing her apart.

She forced herself upright, staggered toward the window with a cigarette already between her fingers by the time she got there. Perched on the sill, one knee to her chest, she sparked the lighter and inhaled deep enough to shake off whatever was still crawling under her skin.

Outside, the sky was eating itself alive: pale gold trying to break through storm-thick clouds and failing. Marti huffed smoke against the glass and watched it smear to nothing.

Typical fucking luck. One bad trip, worse than usual, and now even the weather wanted in on it.

A raindrop hit the windowpane. Then another. The sun fought harder but didn't stand a chance.

She took another drag and let herself think about Pauline for exactly as long as it took for the rain to start streaking desperate little rivers down the glass.

Not like other people; not watching Marti for weakness or waiting for an excuse to scold or save or walk away shaking their head as if they knew better than she did about sinking fast with no intention of swimming up for air.

No, Pauline watched as if she was learning something secret: something fleeting she didn't want to forget before it disappeared. Like maybe Marti wasn't just some inevitable disaster waiting to happen again and again until there was nothing left worth salvaging.

Instead she'd stayed long enough to shove Marti under blankets, as if she had any right pretending to keep someone else safe from anything at all.

The cigarette burned down to its bitter last inch between Marti's fingers before she noticed how long she'd been sitting there thinking stupid shit that never led anywhere good. She stubbed it out against the metal frame and flicked it onto empty pavement below.

She didn't need anyone trying to scrape her off rock bottom with bare hands, not another martyr looking for something broken to fix. But someone who could just be there? Sit in whatever mess this was without making it worse?

Marti laughed once, low and humorless.

Jesus Christ.

One bad trip and now she was catching feelings for the girl who kept her stocked with drugs?

The rain hammered harder against glass, drowning out everything else.

But maybe that wasn't it at all. Maybe Pauline wasn't just "some girl." Maybe.

Nope. Not finishing that thought. Naming something made it real, and real things could hurt you worse than any fucking comedown ever could.

She pushed off the windowsill, restless, and eyed her phone where it sat on the coffee table like a loaded weapon. The real world was there.

Just a little longer. Play it cool, keep some damn distance.

Except she already knew it wouldn't matter how long she waited or how many cigarettes she burned through trying to ignore it.

She was fucked either way, and nothing terrified her more than knowing it wasn't Shadow that had finally done her in this time.

The phone buzzed. Lori.

Sweet, innocent, judgy Lori.

Marti picked up her phone and sent a return message: There in 20.

* * *

"Run that by me again," Lori said, eyes narrowing. "Because I swear to God, you just said the dumbest thing I've ever heard."

Marti stood by the window, watching a cat stretch itself on the fire escape as if it was waiting to trip everyone descending in a hurry. The morning light slanted in behind her. The city beyond the glass didn't feel as heavy today; still full of secrets, still a goddamn mess, but maybe less inclined to crush her outright. Or maybe that was just wishful thinking.

"Thornfield had something new," she said. "A stronger version of Shadow: Golden Shadow. Instead of street fighting his competition, he pulled a good old-fashioned capitalist move. He tried to outsell them." She scratched at her temple, dragging the thought into something sharper. "Maybe he was tired of being number three. Maybe he wanted the fucking crown."

Lori stood close, as usual, and nodded. "He moved product under cover of greasy fries and cheap soda. But you think he was searching out a higher-class market?"

"Yup." Marti flicked open her lighter and pretended to focus on the flame, but they both knew where her eyes landed.

Lori sighed. "Up here," she muttered, tapping Marti's chin with one finger.

"Rude," Marti grinned, lighting up anyway. She took a slow drag before getting back to business. "Follow the money. Evelyn didn't just want a cut. She wanted all of it." Smoke curled toward the ceiling as she exhaled. "Think about it: Thornfield developed Golden Shadow, stronger, nastier, more addictive than anything else out there. He and his wife were at financial odds. But he's dead and Evelyn's got Golden Shadow in play."

"So fast, it's like she had it planned ahead of time," Lori said, voice rising as it clicked together.

Marti pointed at her with the cigarette. "Exactly. His death meant unlimited control: money, formula, lab, network. It's hers now."

"And she needed it to look like suicide," Marti said with a deep exhale of smoke.

"Give the cops an excuse to ignore it without looking obvious."

"But the murder got messy," Marti said. "Maybe she got sentimental for a second. Doubts and all that. Then pulled the trigger." She reached for her glass and took a sip before adding, "And she fucked up. She took the gun in a panic."

"And that made Ari start asking questions," Lori murmured.

Marti nodded once. "Cops bought it. Mayor bought it. Or got paid to buy it. But Stirling? He can't be bought." Another pause before she voiced what they were both thinking: "Evelyn's got friends in high places, and if we don't move fast..." She let that hang in the air between them before finishing, "...our client might wind up dead."

"All this for Golden Shadow?" Lori asked. "What about the blackmail angle?"

Marti ran a tongue along her teeth and remembered: not just the high but the crash at the end of it. The way Golden Shadow didn't let go like the old stuff used to.

"There was something different about that shit," she admitted, voice quiet. "Something dangerous." A pause as a ghost of sensation rippled through her memory like an aftershock from an old wound still healing raw under fresh skin.

"It was beautiful," she finished.

"And then I swear I fucking died."

Lori studied her face like she was looking for cracks in stone.

"Did it taste different?" she asked.

"Nah." Marti exhaled smoke toward the ceiling, eyes narrowed. "Pauline says Evelyn Delacroix handed her the golden inhaler. Why give the hired help a treat like that?" She flicked ash into the tray, rolling the thought around like a bitter pill.

"Because if you like it, maybe you'll become a fucking ambassador?"

"I hardly think my opinion counts for much," Marti laughed.

"Regardless. Gold is money. To entice a higher class of clientele?" Lori asked.

"Which would make any of the competition nervous. Maybe even be the reason to blackmail some of your higher high class clients," Marti said as she pointed at her computer like it would just spit out the answer.

Lori dropped into Marti's chair like she owned it and swiped crumbs and ash off the keyboard with the back of her hand. Marti blew smoke in her face, wishing she was the chair right now.

Lori wrinkled her nose. "Jesus, at least crack a window before we both die of lung cancer."

"Doesn't work like that anymore," Marti grumbled but she obliged, hitching the window open and leaning against the frame as damp air curled around her cigarette smoke.

She aimed her smoke at the cat that had taken refuge under an overhang.

Lori ran her fingers over the keys, settling in as she tunneled through the Dark Web's digital underbelly. The monitor painted her skin sickly blue, shadows shifting across her face while she waded through junk data and dead links: a graveyard of forgotten secrets and bad everything.

After a few blind alleys, she hit gold: a buried chat board marinating in conspiracy theories and half-truths. The posts hinted at something sleek, exclusive; opulence wrapped in whispers.

"Got something," Lori said, leaning closer. "Rumors about Golden Showers."

Marti barked out a laugh. "Golden Showers? Knew you were freaky, but damn."

"Eat shit," Lori shot back, grinning.

The threads stretched back a year: anonymous chatter about a designer strain still in development, engineered for those who didn't just want a high but an experience draped in gold and decadence.

Then Lori's scrolling stopped cold. A post buried deep in the thread made her pulse stutter: a chemical composition laid out in plain text, bold as brass.

She stared at it too long before Marti nudged her boot against Lori's leg. "The suspense is killing me. What's in it?"

Lori exhaled. "The recipe. Listed as Fluorocarbeneoxyridine, FCO-37, and table salt."

Marti raised an eyebrow. "What the fuck is Fluoro-car-bona-whatever-the-fuck?"

"I don't know," Lori admitted, brow furrowing as she ran another search. Silence stretched between them as results loaded. Nothing. "It doesn't exist," she muttered. "Or it didn't." She dragged a hand through her hair, eyes flicking back to the monitor as if reality had shifted when she wasn't looking. "If someone figured out how to make it." She paused. "Then that's the end of your Golden Shadow market."

"Salt?" Marti flicked ash in Lori's general direction. "The fuck does salt have to do with anything?"

"How would I know?"

"You're an engineer. Thought you knew everything."

Lori opened her mouth, shut it, then snapped her fingers. "Wait: halotherapy! Been around for centuries. Salt's supposed to help people breathe better. I bet it's a marketing gimmick. 'Try my Golden Showers and experience the purest breath of your life!'" She grinned.

Marti snorted. "Golden Showers again, huh?" A slow smile curled at the edges of her mouth. "Okay, so Golden Shadow exists, it's addictive, easy to use. Marketed to the rich. Thornfield starts to blackmail the users. But word would spread, put a chokehold on sales. No more money coming in. Evelyn has so much extra product she is giving it away to the hired help. She offs her husband because he was blackmailing clients and--"

"We don't know that Thornfield blackmailed anyone." Lori crossed her arms. "Why would he if he had just created a new product?"

Goddamn woman and her practicality sometimes.

Then Lori spun around, settling between Marti's knees. "Wait! What if Dan Devall killed Thornfield after getting the formula? Wipe out the competition, absorb Thornfield's operation, build his own empire: big enough to challenge Gardner." She dropped her voice to a whisper.

Marti considered that, rolling the thought over like dice in her palm. "With Henry feeding him insider info to crush bad daddy." She exhaled through her teeth. "Consolidate and decapitate."

Lori huffed a laugh. "Jesus, Marti, could you be more dramatic?"

Marti smirked. "Let's hope Gardner appreciates my theatrical talents." Her gaze sharpened as she sat forward.

"You set up a meeting yet? He'll wanna know about Henry."

"Noon. Kentucky Coffee on Third and Main."

Marti groaned. "Fucking coffee shops."

They went over the plan again: Marti would meet with Gardner, show proof Henry was still breathing. The wallet should do nicely. She would gauge if Gardner had sniffed out Devall and Golden Shadow yet. If he had, that might be enough leverage to take straight to Ari Stirling and cash in twice over.

Double payday? Yes please.

It was shaping up to be a damn good day.

At 11:30, Marti slid behind the wheel of her car; at noon, she stepped into Kentucky Coffee and scanned the room. No sign of Gardner yet. Good. She hated keeping clients waiting... especially when they had a habit of killing people.

Allegedly.

Marti slapped a crumpled bill on the counter. Funny how coffee shops and fast food joints all preferred cash. "Black coffee. This big. No sugar, no bullshit." She held her fingers apart to demonstrate, as if she was measuring a fish.

"One no bullshit black," the barista repeated back before swiping the money and keeping the tip.

Marti took her cup to the corner table, dumped a shot of whiskey into it, then drank straight from the flask anyway. The options in front of her sucked. Best-case scenario: Gardner would be happy his son was alive, and Marti walked away with enough cash to patch up what that little shit had cost her; maybe even charge Gardner extra for some SynthoSkin and ViaRevive.

Worst case scenario: Kevin Gardner discovers Henry has not only joined a Devall's gang but was hired to assassinate the private investigator he hired to find his demon seed.

And his son failed, so his son is expendable.

Marti exhaled and thought of something worse: Gardner kills his son for betraying him, Devall hits back at Gardner. Tit for tat war that has Henry as the pawn until Devall finds out Marti told Gardner then it's her neck on the line. The top suppliers in the city get into a full-out war, the city splinters, thousands of innocent people die in the crossfire.

Fun times.

She scrubbed at her face, letting out a curse under her breath.

Back when she was a cop, shit like this didn't happen. Sure, you still had to cross lines sometimes, but at least you knew where they were before you tripped over them.

She checked the time. Gardner was late. She called Lori.

"Where the fuck is he?"

"How would I know? I'm your secretary, not his," Lori shot back. "Although congrats to me. I do know exactly where you are, so job well done."

Marti drained half her coffee in one go, then popped her lips against the rim just to be irritating.

"Marti, he's what? Ten minutes late?"

"I know," Marti grumbled, scanning the shop as if someone was gonna call security on her at any second. "But I fucking hate coffee shops."

"Why? Because there's too many milk alternatives and acoustic guitars?"

"No," Marti whispered, leaning in despite being on the phone. "There are...ugh...normal people here."

Lori scoffed loud enough for Marti to hear over traffic noise on her end. "Tell you what: I'll come keep you company," she said, already out the door by the sound of it.

"No need," Marti said. She wasn't sure she could sit here much longer without losing her mind. She needed something: a hit, a drink, someone to throw up against a wall and finger until they forgot their own name. Not necessarily in that order.

What she did not need was to sit here waiting for Falls City's biggest drug lord like some antsy teenager before prom night.

"I'll be there in ten," Lori said before hanging up on whatever protest Marti might've managed next.

Marti turned over her flask and caught the last drop before shoving it back into her jacket pocket. Well... at least that was one thing checked off her list.

Ten minutes later, Lori strolled in as if she belonged; honestly, she probably did.

Blue dress. Heels. Clutch purse. Lips that could break a lesser woman. Fucking gorgeous.

Marti hated how it made her feel: hot, itchy, and in need of release.

Lori waved at the barista as she slid into the seat across from Marti.

"You know the coffee guy?" Marti asked, narrowing her eyes.

Lori gave her a look usually reserved for people who thought pineapple belonged on pizza. "I signaled my pre-order number." She held up four fingers just as the same smug barista from earlier arrived with a cappuccino and a grin. The little shit placed it down in front of Lori before pivoting on his heel and walking away, but not before tossing a glare Marti's way as if she'd personally offended his ancestors.

"Little fuck," Marti muttered under her breath.

Lori smirked over her cup. "Is that an insult or an invitation?"

Marti shot her a look. "Depends on how good you are under a table."

Lori hummed into her cappuccino, then set it down and studied Marti with something softer in her expression.

Coffee done. Time flew.

Still no Gardner.

That was bad.

Then she saw him.

Not Gardner.

Some idiot in a shitty suit at a small table who kept checking his watch and periscoping like he was waiting for permission to fuck up his own life.

"Oh, for fuck's sake." Marti rolled her eyes so hard she nearly saw the back of her skull. "Hey! Asshat! Over here!" She waved an arm at BadSuit like she was flagging down a cab.

The guy just blinked at her, all wide-eyed confusion.

Marti clenched her jaw and tried again. "You! Move your fucking ass!"

BadSuit finally stood, nerves practically radiating off him as he glanced around at the café's other patrons before shuffling over.

"Marti," Lori hissed, voice low. "What the hell are you doing?"

Marti ignored her, tracking BadSuit's awkward approach. When he got close enough to stink of cheap cologne and flop sweat, she gestured lazily at Lori. "Lori, meet the asshole Gardner sent but was too fucking incompetent to bring a damn photo so he knew who to look for." She turned back to the interloper. "That about right?"

BadSuit grunted. "You Marti?"

"No, I just go around yelling at assholes in cafés for fun." She dragged out a cigarette and tapped it against the table like that might make reality less stupid. "What the fuck is going on?"

BadSuit hesitated, staring down at his hands like they held the answers to life's mysteries. Then: "Mr. Gardner couldn't make it, so he asked—"

"Go fuck yourself." Marti stood up so fast her chair scraped against the floor like nails on a coffin lid. Lori barely had time to grab her bag before Marti stalked toward the door.

"Sorry!" Lori called over her shoulder as she rushed after her, catching up just as Marti kicked the door open like it had personally wronged her. Which, as far as she was concerned, it had.

Outside, Marti made a beeline for her car. "Fucking bullshit games," she muttered under her breath as she yanked open the door and slid inside, shoving an empty inhaler onto the floor without a second thought. The door slammed shut with enough force to rattle the frame. It nearly took off Lori's fingers in the process too.

"Hey! Careful!" Lori shot her an incredulous look before folding her arms and waiting beside the driver's side window as if she had all the time in the world. When Marti refused to acknowledge her existence, Lori knocked on the glass until Marti gave in and rolled it down an inch.

"If Gardner didn't actually send that guy? Good thing we kept our mouths shut," Marti said around a cigarette filter as she pawed through scattered receipts and empty Shadow inhalers for a lighter. "If he did? Then Gardner's a disrespectful prick and he can go fuck himself sideways."

Lori sighed but didn't argue; smart woman.

Then Marti's phone rang. She found the lighter first, lit up slow before answering without checking caller ID. "The fuck do you want, Kevin?"

"My office, Starova." Gardner's voice was all business, no patience left in his tone. "Four-ninety Seventh Avenue." He hung up before she could respond.

Marti exhaled smoke through gritted teeth and chucked her phone at the windshield with enough force to leave matching cracks in both.

"Fuuuuck! That'll cost."

Lori walked around the front of the car (she knew Marti would stay calm as long as she saw her ass) and slid into the passenger seat as if this was just another day ending in Y while Marti threw the car into gear with violent intent.

"You realize your phone probably costs more than fixing your car, right?" Lori said as they peeled away from the curb.

Marti shrugged one-handed and hit the accelerator harder than necessary. "Good thing I'm billing his ass for both."

Chapter 17

Marti ran two reds and cut off a delivery truck, but it wasn't enough. Her hands clenched the wheel as if she could choke the tension out of it. Next to her, Lori had her eyes shut, mouth a thin line of either prayer or regret. Probably both.

Rain hammered down, turning the streets into smeared neon and oily reflections: perfect weather for dealing with Kevin Gardner. Gray, cold, and slick with danger on every corner.

Gardner Enterprises squatted seven stories above the industrial decay of the Grassline District, all smoked glass and brutalist steel. Downtown's towers had money; this one had history. The concrete had once been pristine white. Now it had yellowed like nicotine stains on old fingers. A single brass plaque by the door whispered its name: Gardner Enterprises. No taglines, no explanations. If you needed to know, you already did.

Inside, the place stank of expensive cologne and fresh ink on contracts that would never hold up in court. Marble floors gleamed under too-perfect lighting, bouncing reflections up toward a massive mahogany desk at the center of the room.

Behind it sat a man with blond hair yanked into a bun so tight it looked painful: BunMan, clearly. He was already tracking them before they stopped walking. His gaze flicked from Marti's bloodied boots to Lori's shaking hands, cataloging everything.

Two security meatheads stood like bookends in the hallway beyond him: silent, armed, standing just close enough together to let visitors know exactly where they ranked in the food chain. Bland corporate art clung to the walls as if displaying all the personality of a morgue drawer.

"Starova for Gardner." Marti didn't slow down.

BunMan lifted his hand and the guards shifted forward in sync.

Marti stopped cold.

BunMan barely moved as he said, "We've got a problem already. Let's fix that: your gun."

The guards had been waiting for this part all day. One reached for her piece and Marti didn't fight, not worth broken fingers, but she made him work for it, rolling her shoulders before letting go.

BunMan picked up his phone without looking away from her and pressed a button as if ordering lunch. Three rings later: "Starova for you." He listened, gave Marti another slow once-over, then hung up without a word of confirmation or denial.

Thirty seconds passed, a long stretch of nothing but rain against glass, before another slab of muscle arrived to escort them upstairs.

Marti shook off rainwater as she passed BunMan, getting as close as possible just to piss him off on principle. She followed their guide down halls that were too pristine to be anything but fake wealth on display: the kind bought with receipts that burned under federal scrutiny.

She shot Lori a sideways glance but found nothing but tight-lipped endurance as they walked upstairs and into Gardner's domain.

Kevin Gardner's office sprawled across his building's corner as if he owned not just the space but everything visible through its floor-to-ceiling windows; city lights blinked in sharp reflection against black glass that showed more truth than anyone sitting on this side of his desk ever would. No sneaking up on this bastard. He saw everything coming long before it arrived.

At one end, an imposing desk carved from black walnut claimed its space without apology, flawless save for a lone laptop and a crystal decanter filled with something dark enough to make Marti's mouth water.

Across from it sat two oxblood leather guest chairs placed just too low: a deliberate reminder that anyone sitting there was beneath him before they opened their mouth. Thick rugs softened Brazilian hardwood floors beneath their steps, deadening sound enough to make you wonder if anyone would hear you die.

Behind Gardner's desk hung his only personal touch: an Edward Logic painting depicting a solitary figure at a window, watching something distant, considering something unknowable. A fitting choice for a man who always held more cards than he played.

Marti stepped forward and extended her hand with mock politeness that fooled no one.

"Mr. Gardner," she said as she sank into one of those calculated chairs with zero hesitation. "Nice setup you've got here." A smirk tugged at her lips as she tipped her head toward Lori beside her. "You remember my lovely secretary?"

Gardner glanced at Lori before snapping his attention back to Marti with all the warmth of an executioner reading last rites.

"What the fuck," he said. Not a question. Just a feeling.

Lori settled into her seat while Marti exhaled, letting the attitude skim past her.

She tilted her head at him as if he was some kind of fascinating specimen under glass: something dangerous behind reinforced barriers.

"Why'd you send the loser?" Marti asked.

And then waited to see if he'd lie about it.

Instead, he ignored it.

Gardner leaned forward, elbows on his desk, fingers steepled together as if he thought that made him intimidating. The antique clock behind him ticked, the only sound in the room.

"So?" His voice was sharp. "My son?"

Marti pulled a battered wallet from her jacket and tossed it onto his pristine desk. It spun once before landing face up, a drop of blood standing out like a smoking gun.

"That answer your question?" she said.

"The fuck did you do to my son?" Gardner snatched the wallet, flipping through its contents with too much focus, as if maybe if he turned a twenty over, he'd find a different reality underneath. His jaw tightened when he hit the driver's license.

"Where did you get this?" Voice still measured, but now there was an edge.

Marti sat back, stretching out to make herself comfortable. "Your son's fine," she said. "But finding him just got fifty grand more expensive."

Gardner's nostrils flared. "We had a deal."

"Yeah? Well, deal changed when your precious boy put a bullet in me." She stood, yanked up her shirt without ceremony. SynthoSkin covered her ribs. The pale pink stood out against her paler skin like a bad memory that refused to fade.

Gardner's eyes narrowed as he took in the wound. "My son did that?"

"Damn right," Marti said. "Shot me, beat the shit out of me. Decided he wanted to leave a mark."

Gardner exhaled and sank back into his chair, leather groaning under his weight. He flipped Henry's wallet shut with a snap. "Sounds like Henry to miss," he muttered.

Lori leaned forward before Marti could respond, wrist outstretched; her sleek watch glowed with its holographic display.

"Payment please," she said. Marti could hear the tremor in her voice but she was acting tough.

Gardner tapped his own watch without hesitation. A second later, Lori's device chimed: a tiny ding to confirm fifty thousand crisp shifting hands like it was pocket change.

Marti smiled as she watched Gardner's expression shift; barely perceptible cracks formed in that controlled exterior of his.

Fucking rich boys and their messes.

"You really don't know where your son is, do you?" Marti let the words settle, smooth as glass but just as easy to shatter. "The great Kevin Gardner, who knows every damn thing about everyone, can't even keep track of his own flesh and blood."

Gardner's jaw flexed. "If I knew, I wouldn't have hired you."

"No," Marti said, tilting her head. "It's more than that. You don't know."

Gardner exhaled through his teeth, gaze fixed on the abstract smear of color behind Marti's shoulder as if it held all the answers. "I thought Henry was working with Marcus Thornfield: playing honey pot for rich men, bleeding them dry through Thornfield's racket." His voice dipped lower, almost like he was confessing to himself.

"It was getting dangerous. Some well-positioned men started making noise; blackmail does that. Desperate men do stupid things." He tapped his fingers once against the desk. "Even Mayor Garrison came sniffing around, never said Henry's name outright. He'd been caught up. Wanted Thornfield gone."

Marti sat back and tried to cover her 'I fucking knew it' smile. She knew Gardner had offed Thornfield.

"And what did you say to Garrison?" Lori asked, arms crossed as if she already knew the ending to this story but needed Gardner to say it anyway.

Gardner's laugh had no humor in it. "Told him to handle his own mess. I don't take out competition directly; it's bad business."

So much for that theory.

Marti leaned forward to make him meet her eyes. "And then Thornfield turns up dead anyway."

"Yeah," Gardner muttered, lips pressing into a thin line. "Figured that'd be my son's cue to come home: clean slate and all that." He gestured at her with two fingers. "Obviously didn't happen."

Marti pulled back in her chair, rolling a shoulder as if she could shake off the memory of Henry's bat connecting with her skull. "I found Henry at some warehouse," she said. "That's a lie."

Gardner raised an eyebrow at that, but Marti went on before he could interrupt.

"Lori and I were at the Handsome Dove with Garrison when shit hit the fan."

Gardner's expression sharpened. "Garrison?"

"Yeah," Marti said with a wince as she shifted in her seat, a fresh reminder that her ribs were still sore as hell. She took in Gardner's stare and let him chew on that detail before throwing him another one: "We bolted when the shooting started. Ran straight into Henry instead."

Lori tensed beside her as if she wanted to jump in, but Marti didn't give her the chance.

"His bat found the back of my head before I saw him coming," she said, like it was just another Tuesday night inconvenience instead of a near-death experience. "Woke up in a warehouse after that. So technically, he found me."

Gardner's eyes narrowed to slits. His voice dropped low enough to make Lori stiffen beside Marti. "Isn't the Handsome Dove in Devall's territory?"

"Yep," Marti admitted, keeping her tone light on purpose; she was watching more than listening now because this was where shit got interesting.

"And what exactly was Henry doing in Devall's territory?"

Marti exchanged a glance with Lori before answering with a shrug. "Aside from beating the crap out of me, I don't know. I was there for Garrison. Henry found us."

Gardner drummed his fingers again, processing that little revelation as if he didn't like where it led him but couldn't ignore it either. Then his gaze flicked down to the leather wallet sitting on his desk, the one Marti had pulled from Henry after their little reunion turned ugly.

"Henry had some chemical burns on his hands. Is he a cooker?" Marti asked as she leaned back. She wondered if she should put her boots on the desk.

"No, Henry isn't a cooker," Gardner said with finality.

"Maybe not for you. But those were cooker burns on his arms. Nasty chemical burns."

Fuck it.

Marti put her boots on the desk.

"Get your fucking boots off my desk."

That didn't last long.

"So you met with Garrison in Devall's territory, and Henry showed up to the party?" Gardner asked as he tapped the wallet. "And he shot at you? And beat you? With a bat? With hands with chemical burns, like he'd been cooking?" Gardner asked, too careful for someone who already knew the answer.

Marti stretched out her legs under the table as if she didn't feel the aches settling into her bones. "Beat the shit out of me," she confirmed. She let the next part land clean in his lap: "and I beat the shit out of him right back."She nodded toward the wallet. "He lost."

"You shot him?"

"No, he was the one with the gun. You know, Kevin, he could use some self-defense lessons," Marti said as she reached for her cigarettes.

Gardner didn't react immediately. He turned the wallet over in his hands once more as if he hadn't already committed every scuff and scratch to memory by now. His thumb brushed over something dark near the corner: a stain dried into the leather grain deep enough that it wasn't coming out anytime soon.

His voice was calm when he finally spoke again, but that kind of calm only meant trouble lurking underneath:

"Whose blood is this? Exactly?"

Marti smiled without meaning it, sharp enough around the edges to cut herself open if she wasn't careful.

"Not sure," she said, letting him sit with that uncertainty for a second longer before adding: "Could be mine, could be Henry's... hell, could belong to someone else entirely. It's his wallet, I have no fucking clue what he's been up to."

She leaned in slightly, the way people do when they know they're holding something heavy over someone else's head, but kept her voice near conversational:

"Your boy's running with the wrong crowd, Gardner," she said. Her words carried an edge despite their lightness. "Said he was hired to find me. So whatever game he's playing with Devall? It's bigger than just blackmail now."

The lighter's flame ate the tip of the cigarette as Marti inhaled deeply.

Gardner rose from his chair with a fluidity that belied his age, moving to an ornate bar cabinet nestled between two floor-to-ceiling bookshelves. Crystal decanters caught the light as he opened the cabinet doors.

"Drink?" he offered, his back to them as he selected a bottle of amber liquid. "I find business discussions go smoother with something to take the edge off."

Marti nodded. "Whiskey. Neat." Smoke rolled out of her mouth as she spoke.

"And for you?" Gardner glanced at Lori.

"I don't drink," she replied, her expression unchanged.

Gardner poured a generous measure of whiskey into a heavy crystal tumbler and handed it to Marti before pouring one for himself. He didn't return to his seat, choosing instead to lean against the edge of his desk, looming over both women.

Marti took a sip. "Oh fuck this is good." The whiskey was exceptional: smoky with hints of vanilla and oak, warming her throat with a gentle burn that spoke of age and quality.

"Thirty-year Glen Lach," Gardner said, noting her reaction. "One of life's few genuine pleasures."

He swirled the liquid in his glass, watching the light play through it. "So my son has upgraded from honey pot to hired hit man?"

"He sucks," Marti interjected.

"Maybe someone told him I hired you. So he tried killing my investigator. Probably telling Devall all my secrets." His voice remained calm, but his knuckles whitened around his glass. "That's... disappointing."

My investigator. Fuck.

The silence stretched between them, heavy with implication. Gardner took another sip before meeting Marti's eyes directly.

"I wonder if you'd consider taking on another job for me," he said. "Devall has become a problem. And perhaps Henry too."

Marti set her glass down with a decisive click. "No."

"I'd make it worth your while."

"Devall can't die so soon after Thornfield," Lori said. Both Gardner and Marti had almost forgotten she was there. But indeed, there she was, understanding what was said when it wasn't said at all.

"Two drug kings murdered within days of each other? The police might ignore that. But the Feds would get involved right away."

Gardner's expression remained neutral, but something dangerous flickered in his eyes.

"That would leave you as the last man standing and the obvious mastermind," Marti continued where Lori left off. "Even you don't have enough friends in high places to make that kind of heat disappear."

Gardner's expression softened, the dangerous edge in his eyes receding as he considered the words. He nodded, swirling the amber liquid in his glass.

"You're right," he admitted, his voice carrying a hint of reluctant respect. "That would be... unwise." He took another sip of whiskey, savoring it before continuing. "I appreciate your candor, both of you. Not many people would dare speak so bluntly to me."

Marti shrugged, picking up her glass again. "We aren't most people."

"No," Gardner agreed with a small smile. "You're certainly not." He moved back to his chair and settled into it, the leather creaking beneath his weight. "I like you, Marti, Lorna. You've got guts and brains: a rare combination in this business."

"Lori," she corrected him. Her boldness was rewarded with Gardner's death stare.

"Just doing what you paid me for," Marti replied, though she couldn't help feeling relief. Being on Kevin Gardner's good side was no small achievement in this city.

Gardner's eyes narrowed. "Tell me something. Why was Garrison meeting with you at the Handsome Dove? That's not exactly the mayor's usual haunt."

Marti exchanged a quick glance with Lori before answering. "Apparently, yes it is. He's a regular. I wanted to talk somewhere he thought was safe."

"And what did our esteemed mayor have to say?" Gardner asked, leaning forward.

"He got shitfaced before we got anywhere," Marti said. "Dove told him we were leaving. He came out and Devall's men showed up, shooting at us."

Marti slammed back the last of her drink and put the glass down on Gardner's desk with too much force. "Fuck me."

Both Lori and Gardner shot her a look.

In that moment, the pieces clicked together in Marti's mind. She saw it all, clear as the empty glass in front of her: the timeline, the connections, the dead.

"He did it himself," Marti said, her voice barely above a whisper. She looked up, meeting Gardner's knowing gaze. "Garrison killed Thornfield to end the blackmail. He couldn't get you to do it. He did it and I was investigating. So he hired Devall's people to stop me." Marti jabbed her cigarette toward Gardner. "And it was your son that took the job."

Lori nodded, realization creeping across her face. "And by 'stop,' you mean…"

"Kill me," Marti said, running her finger around the rim of the empty glass. "I was getting too close. Asking too many questions about Thornfield's death. The mayor couldn't have that."

Lori shifted in her seat. "But why not just have Devall's men take Thornfield out from the start?"

Marti let out a sharp, bitter laugh. "Probably turned him down. But he saw us and came right over. Put the pieces together, that I'd been hired to find out who killed Thornfield and poof there we are at the Handsome Dove." She shook her head, disgusted with herself. "He just got too fucking high too fast. Went limp dick before he could do much."

"And when he determined you were dangerous…" Gardner left the thought hanging.

"He made the call to Devall. Right after Dove roused him, probably," Marti said, the scenario unfolding in her mind. "Then followed us out and kept us in the area. Signaling with his fucking watch..."

"To Devall's waiting men," Lori finished.

Marti stood up, adrenaline flooding her system. "And when they didn't get me, Henry stepped in. That fucker has been two steps ahead this whole time. Playing everyone: Thornfield, you, me." She looked at Gardner, her eyes hard.

"And what exactly do you plan to do with this information, Starova?" Gardner asked, leaning back in his chair, studying her with new interest.

"No worries. I don't do cops. I won't share what you told me. The only reason I've said this much is you're part of it. I'm only going to tell my client. Let them decide what to do with it."

"Who is your client? Ari Stirling? Evelyn Delacroix? Patricia Seibert?"

"Lori, send him the address of the warehouse where I left Henry. Thanks for the booze, Kev," Marti said as she walked out the door, Lori trailing behind. She found it interesting that Gardner added the assistant mayor to the list. Was Patricia climbing up the political ladder this way?

Marti approached security first, retrieving her gun with an impatient hand.

Once they were past BunMan, Marti turned to Lori. "Find out where Garrison is. Now."

Lori raised an eyebrow. "How am I supposed to do that? Use a crystal ball?"

"I don't care what your balls are made of," Marti snapped, checking her gun. "Just find him. Tonight, this ends."

Chapter 18

Lori was a genius. She found him and called him.

"Mr. Garrison, we've got the videos. Slip drive. Half a million." Lori leaned against the desk, watching Marti flick ash into an empty coffee cup. She brushed hair out of Marti's eyes.

"No, we didn't make copies. Yes, we watched them. Actually, Marti watched them a lot."

Marti didn't look up from her cigarette. No point denying it.

"But not all. Once we found you, well," Lori continued, "you're not the only star in this little production. Other people, other videos. You can recoup your losses however you want. Half a mil gets you all of it." She paused, letting the silence stretch until a man would sweat. "If not... others will pay."

They arranged to meet at Kransten Park: neutral ground where cartels moved product. Public, with plenty of eyes; none belonging to cops unless those cops had been paid to see nothing.

Kransten Park sat in the middle of Falls City. City Hall to the west, the Redspan District to the north, and thanks to some clever bureaucrat, the Eastside District sat to the east.

They went in wired with cameras, recorders, redundancies on redundancies. The goal wasn't the money. They needed him on tape saying Marcus Thornfield's name, something solid enough to shove in Stirling's face and get paid. And maybe, if they got lucky, avoid a world war.

The rain started as a whisper against the leaves in the park, promising to become something more sinister by nightfall. Marti stood with her shoulders squared, watching Garrison approach through the gathering darkness.

"Hope you don't mind the meeting place we've chosen, Mayor," she drawled, her voice cold as steel. "Though I suppose it's fitting for a man who's made a career of slinking around in shadows."

Garrison halted several paces away, his expensive overcoat catching the faint glow of a distant streetlamp. His eyes narrowed as he studied her face. "I'm surprised to see you in one piece. Last I heard, you were sampling the business end of someone's gun."

"Can't keep a good woman down," Marti replied with a thin smile. "Your hired slinger needs better aim. Or maybe you just need to pay more for quality work."

"I didn't hire them," he said.

"Henry and I talked, Garrison," Marti said. Technically true, though she would never reveal that the talk was almost meaningless.

A muscle twitched in Garrison's jaw as his fingers reached for his watch.

"You touch your watch again, I shoot it off your wrist," Marti said as she pulled her jacket back to reveal her gun. "Hiring Henry Gardner to kill me once: that could be just because I'm an asshole. But twice? Makes a compelling argument that it's because I know you killed Thornfield."

Garrison choked. "What? Murder? That's quite an accusation from someone with no evidence."

"Oh, but I have evidence, the probable cause, a theory of the case," Marti said, nodding toward Lori, who stood at her side. "I have a witness who says you tried to hire Kevin Gardner to take out Thornfield. When he refused, you handled it yourself. Then hired Kevin's son to kill me as I got closer. Clever, trying to set up the Gardner family that way."

"G-Gardner?" Garrison's composure slipped for just a second. "That's absurd."

"What I find interesting," Marti continued, lighting a cigarette, "is the motive. These videos. Frankly, they make me wish I'd brought popcorn and lube."

The ember of her cigarette glowed as she inhaled, illuminating the growing tension in Garrison's face.

"You didn't know you were being filmed, did you? Lori, show the Mayor what we found."

With detachment, Lori produced a phone and tapped the screen. Garrison's eyes shrank at the footage: himself getting fucked by Marcus Thornfield, both faces visible.

"Nothing but consensual sex between adults," Garrison sneered, though the tremor in his voice betrayed him. "This proves nothing."

"From Falls City's most vocal homophobe?" Marti exhaled smoke. "The man who built his political career on 'family values'? The public might disagree."

"Politicians have survived worse."

"Not with multiple videos. Not with what Thornfield was planning to do with them." Marti took another drag from her cigarette. "And certainly not with his murder tied to them."

Rain began to fall more steadily now, drumming against the canopy above.

"You might be surprised by what I know, Bruce."

Garrison's stare flickered, jaw tightening. Marti knew that look. She'd seen it in the eyes of killers weighing their odds, calculating: is there enough to put me away?

She gave him nothing but a slow drag off her cigarette. "Here's the thing. If you didn't tell Gardner to kill Thornfield, you don't have shit to worry about."

She let the words sink in, watching the cracks spiderweb across his careful mask.

"But I've got a witness saying you did. And when Gardner refused, you handled it yourself. Cleaned up your own mess. Then, when I got too close, you hired Devall's men to deal with me."

"You're bluffing," Garrison snapped. Sweat beaded at his temple despite the cold bite in the air. "If you had anything real, Gardner would've taken care of you already."

Marti barked out a laugh, sharp and cold. "Gardner's hands are clean on this one. He's got no reason to come after me." Another drag, another step closer. "Only you do."

Silence stretched between them, broken by a distant siren wailing through empty streets.

"You can't bullshit me, Starova."

"I don't need to." She flicked ash onto wet pavement. "The prosecutor's gonna call it compelling evidence: you killing Thornfield."

Garrison moved fast for a man full of fear and bad choices. His hands shot for her throat, fingers curled like claws. Too bad for him she was faster. Marti dodged sideways, caught his wrist mid-swipe and twisted until bone cracked through the night.

Garrison collapsed against a tree with a strangled curse, cradling his ruined arm. Marti took a step back, shaking out her hand as Lori moved past her, closer than she should've been. Lori Harring had more heart than self-preservation instincts.

"Let me see," Lori murmured, crouching beside him as if he hadn't just tried to kill them both. "You need med-"

Garrison seized her before Marti could react. His good arm yanked Lori tight against his chest, forearm crushing her throat like a steel bar.

"Back off, Starova," he hissed against Lori's ear. "Or I snap your secretary in half."

Lori's eyes locked onto Marti's, wide and furious but steady even with Garrison's grip cutting into her windpipe. Marti didn't hesitate. One smooth motion and she was pulling heat from beneath her jacket; the hammer clicking back cut through the rain.

"Let her go."

"You won't risk hitting her," Garrison sneered, squeezing until Lori choked on air she couldn't take in.

Marti exhaled through her teeth and tilted the barrel, just enough off-center to make a point before she pulled the trigger.

The gunshot split the night apart. Bark exploded from the tree inches from Garrison's skull.

"Jesus Christ!" Lori gasped as he flinched. The second of hesitation was all she needed to slam an elbow back into his ribs and twist free before he could tighten his hold again.

Garrison doubled over with a wheeze as Lori staggered toward Marti, hand pressed against her throat where bruises bloomed across soft skin. Her glare was all daggers when she rasped out, "That was too close."

Marti kept her gun leveled at Garrison's slumped form, adjusting her aim slightly lower this time, aiming for something softer than wood bark but just as likely to splinter on impact.

"Next one goes somewhere less scenic."

The crunch of leaves behind them shattered the moment.

Three uniformed officers materialized from the darkness, their approach masked by the sounds of combat and rain.

Marti's instincts fired. She grabbed Lori's arm. "Cops!"

"My cops!" Garrison's voice rang with triumph. "Get them, boys!"

Marti yanked Lori into motion before the first cop could shout. They tore through the park, feet pounding over wet grass and cracked pavement. The air buzzed with gunfire: sharp, controlled shots, meant to kill.

A bullet took out a chunk of tree bark inches from Marti's head. Another whistled past her ear.

Fuck this.

She vaulted a low retaining wall, her shoulder scraping concrete as she landed on the other side. Lori hit the ground beside her with a grunt.

"This way," Marti snapped, dragging her up again. "Thornfield's zone starts at Addison; we make it there, we might live."

Lori's breath came in ragged gasps, sweat tracking down her face. She was running on fumes. Not gonna last long.

Shadows shifted in the trees to their left. Marti grabbed Lori's collar and yanked them both behind a maintenance shed just as footsteps stormed past. She pressed a finger to her lips and counted three beats before shoving Lori forward again, forcing her legs to move despite the burn screaming up her calves.

The playground loomed ahead: low tunnels and rusting slides that might buy them seconds if they needed cover. A car turned onto the service road nearby, headlights sweeping across damp grass.

Twenty yards to Addison. Fifteen. Ten.

Lori went down hard, her foot catching an exposed root. A sharp cry escaped before she bit it back, but fuck, that was enough noise to get them killed. Marti snagged her jacket and hauled her up like dead weight, pushing her forward as another round of bullets chewed into the dirt behind them.

They exploded onto Addison as if thieves crashing through a storefront window: sudden, loud, desperate. Parked cars became cover; neon-lit sidewalks became salvation. Marti zigzagged between them without pause, lungs burning, until she spotted what she needed: a narrow alley choked with dumpsters and broken glass.

"In there," she barked, shoving Lori into the shadows of a recessed doorway before pressing against the cold metal door herself, chest heaving as if it might break open at the seams. Sweat dripped from her brow. Adrenaline kept her upright when every muscle wanted to fail.

Lori started to speak. Marti clamped a hand over her mouth before sound could undo them both.

Footsteps at the alley entrance.

Heavy.

Deliberate.

Marti's free hand found her gun.

The footsteps hesitated, then moved on. This was Thornfield's territory. They didn't dare.

Marti exhaled and fished out her phone with fingers that trembled just enough to piss her off.

Lori grabbed at Marti's wrist as if she could physically stop this from happening. "Are you sure?" Her whisper was raw against the night air. "Telling Stirling might get Garrison killed."

Marti's laugh had no humor in it. "That bastard has tried to kill us twice! You really think I give a shit?" She let that sink in for half a beat before softening, running a thumb over Lori's knuckles without thinking about it. "I don't want you hurt."

Lori melted into Marti's space as if she belonged there. Not ideal timing for an epiphany like that, but whatever. She whispered, "Can't we go to the cops? There's evidence..." Except there wasn't, not really. Just theory and whispers and one unwilling witness who'd never testify.

No cop would touch this.

Marti pulled away, tearing herself back into reality before she got stupid about it all.

One ring. Two.

Stirling picked up.

"Marti?"

"We need to change the details of our contract."

"What the hell, Starova?" Stirling's voice was sharp, impatient. "What exactly are you selling me?"

Marti drew in cool air, flicking a glance at Lori half-hiding behind her. "This shit is getting me killed. Thornfield's murderer has more power than I thought. If we want him arrested, I need cash: enough to grease the right cops. I want him arrested. Not killed."

Silence stretched between them for a beat. Marti pushed through it. "This way, your hands stay clean. A couple of dumbass uniforms get to make their careers hauling in an asshole on a murder charge."

She could hear Stirling thinking, could feel him weighing the risk against whatever violent fantasy he had planned instead.

"There's a witness. Now, if the witness doesn't testify, and he won't, then the case falls apart," she added. "But the killer's career? That's gone for good."

She had to be precise and truthful enough to do her job, but just crooked enough to prevent another murder.

Stirling let out a bark of laughter, low and dark. "That's cute, Starova. You think I want his job taken away when I can take his fucking life? Who is it?"

Marti clenched her jaw. This was the part she had to win. "An extra hundred grand and you get his name and the evidence," she said, calculating how to make him see reason before his temper took over. "I'll be the one to buy the cops. This will distance you from the whole mess when it goes down."

"Fuck that."

"It's my way or you don't get the information," Marti said. She hoped he would not call her bluff.

"Done." No hesitation this time. Damn it, that was easy. Too easy? "Who is it?"

Marti hesitated. Who was she kidding? Stirling would figure it out soon enough. If she didn't tell him fast enough, he'd assume she was screwing him over instead of keeping them both alive.

"We're in an alley off Vermont and Addison," she said. "The killer sent men after us."

"Stay put, I'll send some men," Stirling ordered, all business now. "How many? Who?"

There were ways to do this gently, to ease into saying Garrison's name so Stirling wouldn't reach for blood. But they were out of time for clever maneuvers like that. Marti swallowed hard and went for blunt force honesty instead:

"Three hired uniforms with guns," she said, pressing herself deeper into the doorway beside Lori as her stomach twisted into knots of unease. Then: "It's Bruce Garrison. The mayor."

Nothing from Stirling's end of the line except dead air thick enough to choke on.

The name hung between them like a loaded gun. Marti's hand trembled against the phone. She'd just signed death warrants. Maybe Garrison's, maybe theirs. Christ, what had she done? Naming him out loud to Stirling was like pulling the pin on a grenade and hoping it only blew up the right people.

"Garrison," Stirling repeated, voice gone flat and dangerous. "Bruce fucking Garrison."

"Listen—" Marti started, but he cut her off.

"No, you listen. That piece of shit has been circling my territory like a vulture for years. You just gave me Christmas morning wrapped in a bow." A pause, then quieter, colder: "My men will handle this properly."

Marti's throat went dry. Properly meant bodies. "Stirling, we agreed—"

"We agreed you'd get money and I'd get a name. You delivered. Now I deliver." She could hear movement on his end, quick footsteps, doors slamming. "Sixty seconds, Starova. My men will be there in sixty seconds."

"Wait—"

But the line was already dead.

Marti stared at the phone in her hand like it might explode. Beside her, Lori's breathing came quick and shallow.

"What did you just do?" Lori whispered.

"I don't know." The admission scraped out of her throat. "Fuck, I don't know."

* * *

Somewhere across the city, in a warehouse that didn't exist on any city planning documents, Stirling's men moved with lethal efficiency.

"Garrison," the tall one said, checking his magazine. "Finally."

His partner, broader and scarred across the knuckles, smiled without humor. "Boss wants this clean?"

"Boss wants this done." The tall one slammed the magazine home. "No witnesses except the ones he specified. The private investigator and her girl are off limits."

"Her secretary," the scarred one corrected, pulling on leather gloves.

"Sure. Whatever helps them sleep at night."

They moved toward the door, a third man falling in behind them. This one carried a bag that clinked softly with each step: tools for making people talk, or making them stop talking forever.

"Remember," the tall one said as they reached their vehicles, "Garrison's been untouchable for too long. Made him sloppy. If we're sloppy, we won't live much longer."

"No worries," the scarred one replied. "I'm never sloppy."

* * *

Back in the alley, Marti's hands wouldn't stop shaking. The weight of what she'd done pressed down on her chest like concrete. She'd been in this business long enough to know the difference between threat and execution, and she'd just orchestrated the latter.

"We need to move," Lori said, tugging at her sleeve. "Marti, we need to—"

"No." Marti pulled her deeper into the shadows. "Stirling's men are coming. We run now, we're dead. We stay put, we're under his protection."

"Protection?" Lori's laugh came out cracked. "You just told a crime boss that the mayor or another crime boss or whatever the fuck he is, killed his boss. That's not protection, that's being witnesses to a fucking massacre."

Marti lit a cigarette with trembling fingers. "Welcome to how I stay alive in this city."

But even as she said it, doubt gnawed at her. She'd walked a tightrope for years, playing all sides, keeping the balance. Tonight she'd taken a machete to that rope. Garrison would be dead within hours, maybe minutes. His blood would be on her hands as surely as if she'd pulled the trigger herself.

"I should have found another way," she muttered.

"Can you still call the cops? Promise the money?"

Marti laughed, but there was no humor in it. "I'm going to try."

Footsteps echoed past the alley's entrance, slow and deliberate. Marti shoved Lori behind her, heart hammering as she scanned every dark spot between them and the streetlamp. A shitty place for a last stand if this went sideways.

Then movement. A shadow breaking away from the night itself.

Marti aimed her gun and cocked it.

A deep voice cut through the tension like a blade to the throat: "Stirling sent us."

For one agonizing second, Marti wasn't sure if relief or raw survival instinct would win out, if this was another trick or a goddamn miracle, but then heavy boots scuffed closer and figures stepped into view: armed, sharp-eyed men whose presence alone shattered whatever grip terror had on them just moments before.

Lori sagged against Marti with something close to relief; Marti let herself breathe again, just once, before straightening up and rolling her shoulders back as Ari Stirling's men closed ranks around them like a fucking wall made of muscle and gunmetal certainty.

A barrier between them and whatever nightmare still lurked beyond that alleyway's edge.

Gunfire cracked in the distance, sharp and final. A few voices shouted, then cut off. A phone rang. One of Stirling's men answered, grunted something low, then turned to them.

"Time to go."

Marti and Lori didn't argue. They pushed off the cold wall and followed, stepping out of the alley into sickly yellow streetlight. The black sedan waiting for them looked as if a politician would get executed in it. Tinted window rolled down slow, deliberate. Stirling's face emerged from the shadows, all teeth and amusement.

"Marti," he said, smooth as oil. "You've done excellent work. Tell me more about how you know." Beat. His head tilted. "What's your proof?"

She motioned for Lori with her head. "She'll send everything over. The evidence is solid. We all know the stakes here." Marti lit a cigarette off shaking fingers and exhaled. "Garrison asked Gardner to kill Thornfield. Gardner refused. He's your witness," she said. "Motive was blackmail, sex tapes included."

Stirling laughed, low and knowing. Not surprising.

"How'd you end up at Gardner's?"

Marti flicked ash onto the curb instead of answering directly. "Different case."

"Fucking brilliant. Only you could talk to Garder and to me and still be alive. I like you," Stirling said like that was an acceptable compliment. But Marti had zero fucks left to give about his feelings on the matter.

"You know Gardner won't testify, but he'll confirm with you. Probably," she said, meeting his gaze head-on through the haze of streetlight and smoke. "And when he says he turned Garrison down? I believe him."

Stirling considered her for one long moment, then reached for something beside him in the seat: a thick white envelope wrapped tight with a red rubber band like a wound stitched shut.

Cash. Untraceable as a ghost and twice as useful. Marti barely had time to process the payout.

"Evelyn will be very pleased," he muttered, tossing it out the window like a man flicking breadcrumbs to pigeons. "Finders keepers. Good luck."

Lori snatched it midair like a starving thief and tucked it into her jacket with hunger. She knew if Marti got her hands on it, it would go up in smoke.

Stirling smirked at that: the kind of smirk that could cut glass if you let it settle too long on your skin. "Your girlfriend's smart."

"She's not my girlfriend," Marti shot back before she could think better of it. "She's my secretary."

Stirling nodded once in return before leaning back toward them with assurance: "You've got no more concerns about the men chasing you."

The window slid back up like a reverse guillotine blade, cutting them off from whatever else he might've said if he'd cared enough to linger. Both vehicles peeled away from the curb while their personal escorts dissolved into whatever shadows they came from without a backward glance.

Silence stretched thin between them until Marti exhaled through her teeth and slapped at her pockets as if she might lose her mind otherwise.

"Jesus fucking Christ. Left front pants pocket," Lori supplied without prompting, arms crossed over that fat stack of bribe money as if keeping score of who owed who what now.

Marti found her inhaler exactly where Lori said. She popped off the cap, took one quick hit, then let her shoulders sag loose against exhaustion's creeping edge at the chemical relief flooding her bloodstream like salvation itself.

"What happens now?" Lori asked after a beat, voice soft but still laced steel-thread strong beneath all its quiet understanding of how deep this shit ran between them now.

Marti tapped two fingers against the envelope still tucked under Lori's elbow in silent instruction before answering: "Now we put that in the safe while I figure out which cops are honest enough to make an arrest but dirty enough to need convincing first."

Lori glanced down at the package. She tilted her head toward an empty side street shrouded in morning quiet too heavy not to feel unnatural. "Car's back that way," she murmured more than announced, but Marti caught every ounce of meaning packed into those few syllables anyway: I'll handle this part while you do you.

And just like always, like every time before this one, Marti let her go without argument she didn't have energy left to fight for anymore tonight anyway.

She flicked her hand, dismissive, and Lori walked back toward the car. With one hundred grand in her hands. Safer now than she had ever been in her whole life.

Or so they both wanted to believe.

Chapter 19

Marti slid the rod through her gun barrel in the dim light of her studio apartment.

She'd fired once, twice in the park. Two shots that meant nothing. Now her hands worked automatically, cleaning away the evidence of panic, of fear. Not for herself; never for herself.

Click. Snap. Lock.

The gun came together as her thoughts fell apart.

The rain started sometime after midnight, the slow, lazy kind that tapped at the window like a drunk lover who forgot their keys. Marti slouched in the battered armchair by the radiator, one boot propped on the windowsill, the other planted firm on the whiskey bottle beside her. It was cheap shit: good enough to burn, not good enough to savor. She didn't drink for taste anyway.

One pill left.

The Fentafill sat on her palm, tiny and white and full of promises. There'd been a time when she hesitated before swallowing one of these. That time had passed. She dry-swallowed it then chased it with a sip of whiskey, let her head fall back against the chair, and waited for it all to stop feeling so goddamn real.

Somewhere under the mess of cigarette packs and junk mail on her table sat her Smart-Paper pad, her own notes about the Marcus Thornfield's case file. Motive and opportunity tied together in sex and money.

Stirling had put down good money for answers, and she had given him every last one.

Bruce Garrison killed Marcus Thornfield.

Ari Stirling wanted Bruce Garrison dead for it.

Marti Starova made that connection and now had to call some dirty honest cops to make it all make sense.

She closed her eyes and tried to conjure up regret. It didn't come easy.

Maybe it mattered once: who pulled which trigger, who made which call. But now? Now it was just math. One murder begets another. One job leads to one corpse, and so on until someone with more money or less patience decides it's time to wipe the whole slate clean. She wasn't going to lose sleep if a killer got killed.

But she wasn't sleeping either.

She reached for her cigarettes and came up empty-handed. Somewhere between the alley and now, she'd smoked through her entire pack without noticing.

She ran a tongue over the inside of her cheek, tasting old tobacco and worse decisions, then leaned forward, slowly, to fish through the pocket of her coat hanging off the chair across from her bed. The motion made the room tilt as if an old car was taking a turn too wide, but she found what she needed: a crumpled pack with maybe one left inside if luck still existed in this world.

She lit up, took a drag deep enough to scrape against her ribs, and exhaled toward the ceiling where damp stains curled like inkblots across yellowed plaster. What did they look like tonight? A cat arching its back? A man getting shot? A little girl with her heart ripped out?

Did she care?

Not in any way that mattered anymore, but something kept poking at her ribs from the inside out, as if broken glass lay under skin.

Thornfield hadn't been good people; not even close. But killing him hadn't balanced any moral scales either. He was just another corpse dropped into an overflowing graveyard of bad men with worse enemies. Now Garrison was next in line because she had made sure his name was written down in bloodied ink. Otherwise it would be written in pencil smudges that could be erased away by bribes or time or power.

Marti rubbed at her temple with two fingers as the pill started sinking its teeth in deep, the numbness creeping through muscle and bone like molasses poured over rusted steel wiring.

She thought about calling a cop honest enough to go through legal channels instead of burying the story. But who? The city wasn't built for saints like that anymore; hell, maybe it never had been. The ones willing to take bribes weren't about to stick their necks out on this kind of job unless they got something better out of it than hush money and their names in the paper. Marti didn't have anything better left to give except maybe herself, and that wasn't worth shit anymore either.

She pulled the Smart-Pad from beneath the crap and flipped it open, just for something to do, just for some excuse not to think too hard about what came next.

Marcus Thornfield's dead-eyed mugshot stared back at her as if he knew how this all ended before she even put pen to paper.

She grunted and slammed the folder shut again.

Garrison would die because Marti did what she was paid to do.

That was his problem now. Maybe he had enough cops in his pocket and friends in high places to get out from under this, to protect him. Maybe.

She reached for the whiskey again, tipped back another mouthful that burned worse than guilt ever could.

Tomorrow morning she'd wake up hungover with nothing solved except what she'd known all along:

There's no justice here, just survival.

And survival didn't give a damn about right or wrong.

Marti picked up the phone and dialed. Schaefer. Park. Huber. Padilla. All honest cops. None answering.

As if someone had called ahead with a warning: Don't talk to Starova.

Marti felt a pang of disappointment. She'd need the light of day (yeah right, light) and Lori's help to track a federal agency to arrest Garrison. There was nothing left to do tonight.

Marti collapsed on the bed but her mind would not rest.

Marti's thumb hovered over the phone screen. One call. That's all she owed him. Maybe not even that. The fucker had tried to have her killed.

She took a shallow breath, the weight of the phone suddenly heavy in her palm. Bruce was alive right now. Probably not for long.

The same old dance. She'd warn him, he wouldn't listen, but at least she could sleep knowing she'd tried. It never worked, but these ritual warnings were the last thread keeping her tethered to something like humanity.

Before logic could intervene, she punched in his number.

Ring. One. Two.

"Yeah?" Garrison's voice came through relaxed, almost lazy. Television murmured in the background.

"Listen up, you stupid shit." Marti kept her voice low, each word a blade. "Stirling's coming for you. Tonight. You've got maybe an hour to run or you're dead."

The line went quiet. She could hear him breathing, processing. Her phone chimed with an incoming request.

Video chat? Seriously? She hesitated, then tapped accept.

Garrison's face filled the screen: stubble-rough and whiskey-flushed. He sat in his kitchen, empty beer bottles standing like sentinels behind him. A television flickered blue shadows across the wall.

"Marti Starova?" He laughed, a sound like gravel shifting. "How the fuck did you even… never mind. What the hell are you talking about?"

"I'm talking about Marcus Thornfield with a bullet in his body and Ari Stirling wanting to balance the books." She leaned closer to the screen. "You killed his boss, Bruce. Do the fucking math."

"Stirling?" Another laugh, looser this time. He tilted a beer bottle to his lips, throat working as he swallowed. "Christ, you're paranoid. Stirling doesn't even know I exist."

"He knows now."

"Says who?"

Marti's jaw tightened. She stared directly into the camera, letting the silence stretch until it snapped. "Says the person who told him."

On screen, Garrison's expression transformed. The smirk vanished, confidence draining away like water down a gutter.

"You what?"

"I did my job." Her voice remained steady while her free hand curled into a fist against her thigh. "I found Thornfield's killer. I reported back to my client. That's how this works."

"Your client." His voice flattened. "Stirling was your client."

"Yeah."

"And you just… you sold me out?"

"Call me Judas. I gave him what he paid for."

"Jesus Christ, Marti." His face twisted, something raw flickering across it. "I thought you were…" He stopped, squared his shoulders, leaned back in his chair with manufactured casualness. "Doesn't matter. Stirling's a businessman, not a psychopath. We can work something out."

"No, you can't."

"Sure I can." His fingers drummed against the beer bottle. "I've got money, connections. Hell, maybe I can even convince him Thornfield had it coming. That he's better off."

Through the video, Marti noticed the kitchen window behind him. Black glass reflecting nothing but Bruce's kitchen. The street outside was dark, quiet. In Falls City, quiet streets were never a good sign.

"Bruce, listen to me." She leaned closer, lowering her voice. "Run. Right now. Don't pack, don't call anyone, just fucking run."

"Relax, sweetheart." He raised the beer bottle in a mock toast, lips curving into that smirk she'd once found charming. "I've been in this game longer than you know. I know how to handle—"

The crack of splintering wood cut through his words.

The video image lurched wildly as Garrison spun around. The phone tumbled, bouncing across a surface. Marti caught disjointed images. A chair overturning, beer bottles rolling across tile, Garrison's legs backing away from something beyond the frame.

"What the fuck?" His voice sharpened with sudden panic. "What is this?"

Marti shook her head. She'd just fucking told him.

Heavy footsteps thudded through the speaker. Multiple sets. The phone had landed at an angle where she could see part of the room. Garrison's shadow stretching long against the wall, other shadows converging toward him.

"Bruce Garrison?" A voice Marti didn't recognize. Flat, professional. Cold.

"Look, if this is about money—"

"This is about Marcus Thornfield."

"Wait, we can talk about this. I've got cash, I've got—"

"Ari says hello."

Two gunshots cracked through the speaker, sharp and final. The phone's speaker buzzed with the concussion as the video feed trembled.

The phone spun again, landing face-down on linoleum. The screen went dark, but the audio continued. Footsteps retreating, murmured voices, a door slamming shut.

Then nothing but the hollow sound of an empty room.

Marti disconnected the call, her heartbeat steady despite the tremor in her fingertips. She prayed those bastards wouldn't think to check his recent calls.

She'd eat the sim card if she needed to.

She stared at the blank screen, feeling the weight of what she'd just witnessed settle into her bones. Outside her window, Falls City continued its nocturnal rhythm. Traffic lights changed, music thumped from distant clubs, people lived their oblivious lives. Across town, Bruce Garrison lay cooling on his kitchen floor because he'd thought himself smarter than the game they all played.

Marti set the phone down with deliberate care and reached for the whiskey bottle. Some nights required chemical assistance to keep the ghosts at bay.

Chapter 20

In the morning, having nowhere else to go, Marti headed to her office.

She shoved the door open with her shoulder, coffee in one hand, cigarette in the other. Her hoodie stayed up despite the clear lack of rain indoors. She still couldn't think with her head pounding from last night. Sobriety had done nothing to dull the raw edges scraping at her skull.

Lori was at her desk, typing as if they hadn't almost died together less than twelve hours ago, as if she hadn't stood shoulder to shoulder with Marti, staring down death, and then just gone home and slept it off.

Marti envied that.

"You smell like shit," Lori said without looking up.

"Feel worse." Marti dropped into her chair, which protested with a creak. "Tell me something good."

"You're alive."

Marti exhaled smoke toward the ceiling. "Allegedly."

Lori looked over, eyes sweeping across Marti's disheveled appearance: clothes wrinkled from yesterday, shadows under her eyes pronounced enough to be bruises. "Did you sleep?"

Marti took a sip of coffee that tasted like regret and burned beans. "Define sleep."

Lori shook her head, but if she had an opinion about Marti's choices, she kept it to herself. "The money is safe."

That got Marti's attention. She straightened. "And?"

"That's it. Just waiting."

Marti hummed but didn't press it. That was the thing about Lori: she let silence talk when it needed to.

The office smelled of rain from where someone, probably Lori, had cracked the window open. The world outside was moving on, people going about their lives as if last night hadn't happened, as if guns hadn't been drawn and blood hadn't nearly been spilled.

"Did you call them?" Lori asked after a stretch of quiet.

Marti took another drag of her cigarette instead of answering.

Lori sighed. "They aren't going to help?"

"Everyone was out at two in the morning." Marti stubbed out what was left of her cigarette and started rolling another one. "We need to track down a federal agency that can handle this."

Lori studied her for a beat, then shook her head with a small smile that made something twist in Marti's chest.

God she was beautiful.

"Agreed," Lori said, turning back to her computer. "Let me figure out who will have jurisdiction."

Marti flicked ashes onto the floor. The phone calls could wait. She wasn't ready for whatever brand of bullshit the cops would sling at her this morning.

"Did our run-in last night make the news?"

"Lemme check," Lori said as she switched from one screen to another.

Marti leaned over Lori's desk, scanning the screen. "Bigger news."

Garrison's death was plastered across every news site in Falls City. Mayor Found Dead at Chata Falls. The headlines all said the same thing: an accident, a tragic misstep.

Marti's stomach clenched like a fist. A cold sweat broke across her forehead as she read the details. The same bullshit packaged in official language. Her hands trembled slightly, not from withdrawal but from rage. The same corrupt system, the same lies, the same bodies washing up while the powerful stayed dry.

"Goddamn it," she whispered, her voice like gravel. "We warned him. We fucking warned him."

She slammed her palm against the wall, the dull thud echoing in the small office. The pain felt good—real—unlike the sanitized fiction playing out on the screen.

"Yeah, sure. Just like Thornfield slipped on a bullet."

Lori's face had gone pale, her lips pressed into a thin line. Her hands shook as she clicked through another article. "It says there were no witnesses." Her voice cracked on the last word.

"There never are when powerful men die." Marti pushed away from the desk, rolling her shoulders, trying to shake off the weight pressing on them.

Lori's eyes welled up suddenly, tears spilling over before she could catch them. She turned away, swiping angrily at her cheeks.

"Hey," Marti said, softer now, crossing to her side. "Hey."

"We could have—" Lori started, then stopped herself. "I know we tried. I know we did everything we could. But he's still dead."

Marti crouched beside her chair, not touching her but close enough that Lori could feel her presence. "This isn't on us."

"I know," Lori said, meeting Marti's eyes. "I don't blame you. God, after what you risked last night..." She shook her head. "I just hate this system sometimes. My dad was a cop for thirty years and he'd be disgusted by what happened here."

Marti tentatively placed her hand on Lori's arm. The contact sent electricity through her fingertips. "Your dad raised a good one."

Lori covered Marti's hand with her own, her thumb tracing small circles against Marti's skin. The moment stretched between them, fragile and charged.

"You did everything you could," Lori said finally, her voice steadier. "More than anyone else would have done."

Marti didn't know how to respond to that, to someone having faith in her, so she just nodded, squeezing Lori's arm once before pulling away.

Lori hesitated before speaking again. "Do you think..." she swallowed, then tried again. "Do you think this is over?"

Something about the way she asked made Marti stop. Over? They'd uncovered a murderer, tied up loose ends, seen justice meted out in the city's usual underhanded way; but nothing ever ended in Falls City. The names changed, but power stayed where it always had: just out of reach.

Marti rubbed a hand over her face. "I think it's as over as it's gonna get."

Lori studied her before nodding. Then, with that mischievous glint back in her eye: "My therapist knows all about last night, by the way."

Marti arched a brow. "Yeah?"

Lori leaned back in her chair, stretching her arms overhead, pretending like she wasn't watching Marti's nipples get hard. "Mmhmm. She said it was a classic case of unprocessed trauma wrapped in reckless heroics."

Marti snorted. "That what they're calling it these days?"

"And," Lori continued, smirking now, "she suggested I explore my coping mechanisms with someone I trust."

Marti gave her a long, measured look. "And by 'explore' you mean..."

Lori grinned. "Dinner. Obviously."

Marti shook her head, exhaling smoke towards the ceiling. "Obviously."

"So?" Lori twirled a pen between her fingers. "Know anyone I can trust?"

Marti took another drag from her cigarette, then flicked away the ash. She let the silence stretch until Lori squirmed before saying:

"You can trust me to fuck up."

Lori laughed, reaching for the ringing phone. "Baby steps, Marti. Baby steps."

Marti barked a laugh, shaking her head as Lori grinned.

The city outside kept moving, uncaring of who lived or died last night. Cars weaved through traffic; neon flickered on signs advertising dreams no one could afford. Falls City didn't mourn its dead for long.

Marti stepped back into her office, leaving the door half-open: a compromise.

She dropped into her chair and turned the inhaler of Shadow between her fingers before setting it beside an ashtray overflowing with yesterday's almost-death.

A cough.

Lori leaned against the doorway, arms crossed, eyes sharp with something unreadable.

"Well," Lori said, "you're gonna love this."

Marti didn't look up. "Doubt it."

"New client. Wants to hire you to investigate a suicide."

Silence settled between them like a held breath.

Marti exhaled before meeting Lori's gaze. There was something there. Understanding, maybe. The knowledge that someone else saw her, really saw her, and still stuck around.

"No."

Lori smirked as if she'd been expecting that. She straightened, took a deep breath, composing herself before returning to her desk. She lifted the receiver to her ear and said with perfect professional calm:

"She says go fuck yourself."

She hung up.

Their eyes met across the office, and something passed between them. An acknowledgment of what they'd survived, what they'd seen, what they still might be to each other.

Marti took another drag of her cigarette and watched smoke twist toward the ceiling, fading like a ghost.

Outside, car horns blared. A siren wailed, distant and irrelevant.

Tomorrow waited beyond the window's neon glow: more bodies, more lies. But right now?

Right now was enough.

She reached for the Shadow and took a hit.

Drugs. Sex. Murder.

They were all just different ways to disappear.

Continue the Falls City Series

What happens next? Find out in: ***Shadow Work*** – Coming September 26, 2025
In Book 2 of the Marti Starova Thriller series, PI Marti Starova is back and the body count is rising. From dead dealers to corrupt cops, Marti puts it all on the line to find the killer and the truth.

◆

Rain-Soaked – Coming November 5, 2025
Almost - Coming January 16, 2026
The Familiar Dark - Coming March 11, 2026

Ready to keep reading? Pre-order now!